KU-315-849

HER MARRIAGE SECRET

BY
DARCY MAGUIRE

MILLS & BOON®

All the characters in this book have no existence outside
the imagination of the author, and have no relation
whatsoever to anyone bearing the same name or names.
They are not even distantly inspired by any individual
known or unknown to the author, and all the incidents

All rights reserved. The text of this publication
or any part thereof may not be reproduced or transmitted in any form or by any means, electronic or mechanical, including photocopying, recording, storage in an information retrieval system,
or otherwise, without the written permission of
the publisher.

DONCASTER LIBRARY AND
INFORMATION SERVICE

019338231

CHI   8·1·03
         £12·80

MILLS & BOON and
MILLS & BOON with the Rose Device
are registered trademarks of the publisher.

First published in Great Britain 2002
Large Print edition 2002
Harlequin Mills & Boon Limited,
Eton House, 18-24 Paradise Road,
Richmond, Surrey TW9 1SR

© Debra D'Arcy 2002

ISBN 0 263 17383 6

Set in Times Roman 16½ on 18½ pt.
16-1202-45038

Printed and bound in Great Britain
by Antony Rowe Ltd, Chippenham, Wiltshire

HER MARRIAGE
SECRET

PROLOGUE

THE house was dark.

Jake quickened his pace, tightening his grip on his case as he moved through the shadows. She should be home. It was too early to be asleep. An unusual time to be shopping. She wouldn't be out on a Tuesday night…

His heart hammered in his chest, drumming against his ribs, deafening his thoughts as he fumbled for the keys.

He paused. Took a deep breath. Plucked the right key from the bunch and shoved it in the lock.

Jake pushed open the door and felt the cold emptiness of the house envelop him. Fear gripped him. Where was she?

He moved quickly through the house, flicking the switches, flooding the rooms with light. The place was neat, cool, tidy. He swiped a finger along the kitchen bench and examined the fine layer of dust on the tip of it. Jake shuddered.

He yanked his mobile from his belt and punched Danny's number. The painful knot of fear in the pit of his gut swelled with every ring.

'You're back,' Danny said.

'Where is she?' His voice cracked.

A pause. 'I'll come round.' And Danny rang off.

Jake dialled again, getting a message service. What the hell was going on? What couldn't Dan tell him over the phone?

He ran a hand through his hair. If something had happened to Meg, Danny could have rung him. He always had his mobile with him. Icy fingers squeezed his chest. Why the hell hadn't Danny rung him?

Jake clenched his fists by his sides. She was his life, his reason for being. What the hell had happened? He snatched the phone book up and slammed it onto the bench, rifled the pages for hospitals.

'You won't find her in there.' Danny's voice was slow and gentle.

Jake swung around. Danny stood in the doorway, his hands in his pockets, his shoulders hunched, his face dour.

'What is it? What's happened to Meg? Where is she?'

'She's gone.'

Gone. His legs shook under him and he sank into the nearest chair. 'What do you mean gone? Gone where? How?'

'She left you three weeks ago.'

'What?' His voice broke and he covered his mouth with his hand, rubbing his bristles. This couldn't be happening. Not to them. Not to him. Not after all he knew. He was never going to muck up his life like his parents had.

'She packed up and left you.'

'I don't understand.' The words choked him. He did everything right, didn't he? Sure, he was away a lot. He was working hard for the security of owning their own home. Which was more than his own father ever had…half-sloshed in the front lounge and out of work until he walked out the door one day and didn't come back.

Danny touched him on the shoulder. 'She didn't love you, mate, that's all.'

'That's all?' The words burst from his throat. How could it be? They were like music together. His loins heated at the memory of her.

'You shouldn't have swept her off her feet like that, so soon after her dad dying and all.' Danny stalked to the door. 'You didn't deserve her.'

Jake lifted his head.

'You weren't good enough for her, mate.' Danny stood tall and rigid, glaring at him. 'You took her at a vulnerable time but now she's woken up to her senses. She wants a life that doesn't include you.'

'How do you know that?'

'Apart from being here when you weren't?' He shifted his weight and looked at the floor. 'Because *I* love her.'

'What?' Jake stood up and reduced the distance between them in a heartbeat, his blood surging with fury.

Danny quailed. 'I didn't tell Meg. Truly, I didn't.' He looked to the door. 'I wish I had.'

Pain branded Jake deep in the chest. 'Get out!'

The man who had been his best mate for as long as he could remember turned away from him like a stranger and melted into the shadows.

Jake blindly stumbled to the mantelpiece, his breath coming harsh and hard. He reached out, touching the photos, tracing Meg's smiling eyes, her soft lips, her silky blonde hair that used to drape over his chest as she slept.

So he wasn't what she wanted.

Regrets assailed him. Yes. He'd done a lot wrong. Too fast. Too busy. Too blind. He looked to the door and it was all he could do not to go after her. But it wouldn't change anything. He was still the man he was.

Jake sat in lonely silence, his thoughts jagged, painful. A bitter battle raged between his own desires and the needs of the woman he loved with all his heart and soul.

There was only one decision to make. He was going to become his own man, become more civilised, become the man that would win Meg's heart. And then he'd find her, make her his…and never let her go.

CHAPTER ONE

'Wow, would you get a load of that one?' Suzie gestured wildly. 'He's a 9.9 on the male Richter scale!'

Megan James turned in her seat and smiled at her best friend's enthusiasm. She scanned the busy Melbourne restaurant obligingly, perusing the suited men that crowded the place. Suzie sure knew how to pick restaurants for single women to have lunch in—there had to be at least ten men for every woman, and the added bonus of the very virile, handsome Italian waiters.

'The tourist.' Suzie pointed to the well-built man at the bar.

His casual attire made him stick out among the businessmen. He was tall, broad-shouldered, slim-hipped and long-legged. A tailor's delight. It would have been nice to design that shirt and trousers around *his* body.

A warm tingle caressed her spine. He certainly radiated 'wrap your arms around me'. Meg sighed. So he had a nice body, but nothing outstanding she could see that would elicit such a response from Suzie—except his taste in clothes. But then, she couldn't see his face.

Suzie nudged her. 'Well?'

Meg shrugged and pushed a strand of her short blonde hair back from her face. 'I can't even see him properly. He could have a face like—'

He turned towards them as if on cue. His vivid green eyes scanned the room with a casual indifference.

Meg's stomach clenched tight. He was clean-shaven, his strong jawline giving his features a power that she'd forgotten. His dark hair was cut short now, but there was no mistaking him; his ruggedly handsome face was all too familiar.

Meg grabbed the menu she'd left idle in front of her and slapped it to her face, her heart thudding fiercely.

'What are you doing? Have you gone crazy, Meg?'

'We've got to get out of here,' she whispered shakily from behind the menu. Meg's mind tumbled around in confusion. How could he have found her after all this time? It had to be coincidence.

Desire pulsed hot through her veins, bringing a deep low ache to her body, enticing her mind into fantasies of what they'd shared once, long ago.

Damn him. She was still as disturbed by him as she had been three years ago. And now he was here. She shook off her body's traitorous response. She'd always told herself that if he came looking for her it would be out of obligation, but as the days, weeks and then months had gone by, and he hadn't turned up, she'd concluded soberly that she hadn't meant anything to him. She'd been a notch for his ego with a dose of obligation thrown in—nothing more.

'Why?' Suzie sounded bewildered. 'Don't you like him? You'd look great together, and he's definitely loaded. He's perfect for you.'

'Believe me, he's not.' Meg lowered the menu slightly to see her over-zealous friend ogling the man she could only label as an ordeal personified. The man who had sent her whole life awry.

'Come on, Meg. Gosh, you sound like some old prude. He looks like the perfect stranger to me.'

He's not a stranger—and he's far from perfect! she wanted to yell. For years Meg had fostered a crush on him. Years of teenage fantasies about the boy next door falling in love with her. Time had dragged by until the day when he'd come back from overseas and had set to seducing her. It had been all her dreams come true and she'd been so keen to believe every word he'd uttered, every touch and every kiss.

Blood pooled in her cheeks. He hadn't needed to try very hard. She'd been a young, naive idiot to think there could've been anything between them—anything serious, anything that would stand the test of time.

'Come on, Meg. You're being silly.' Suzie cast a long look in his direction.

Meg could see the admiration in Suzie's eyes. Almost a mirror of what she must have looked like years ago. She slapped Suzie on the arm. 'With a look like that he'll come over!' If he did she'd just die. How could she look at him after all that had happened between them? Guilt assailed her. For the running, for the hiding, and for the secret that hung heavily in the base of her stomach.

Suzie frowned. 'That's the point. You've got to get a guy in your life. There's more to life than work. I could go over and get him to—'

Meg's hand flew out and grabbed Suzie's wrist. 'Don't you dare!' The look of shock on her friend's face snapped her back to reality. 'I'm sorry.' She tried to slow her breathing. 'I know him, okay, and it didn't work out.' That was an understatement!

Suzie recovered quickly. 'Can I go over, then, and have a go at him?' She pulled her long auburn hair over her shoulders, arranging it over her chest to look as though she had just fallen out of a fashion magazine. 'Could you introduce me? What's his name?'

'No, you can't go over.' A wave of unfamiliar emotion swept over her. She froze. She couldn't still feel for him? After all the pain he'd caused her? After all this time?

Meg gritted her teeth. She was annoyed at her idiocy. It was over, she proclaimed to herself—as she'd done many times before. So Suzie was welcome to him. As long as she didn't bring him anywhere near her.

'Jake.' His name slipped from her lips. A name she'd scrawled over her textbooks, over her heart. Etched in, refusing to budge no matter how much she had tried to rid his memory from her life. 'His name is Jacob.'

Jacob. The young boy next door who had intruded constantly on her time with her father. Her father's dust-covered four-wheel drive would pull up in the driveway and Jake would be over the fence and next to Dad in a flash. She'd hated him at first—stealing her father's attention, listening to her dad's exploits in

New Guinea, in Saudi Arabia and in the Australian outback with more enthusiasm and gusto than she could manage. He would gasp about the monstrous earth-moving equipment Dad had worked around and brag how he would do the same when he grew up. Her dad had loved the attention.

The gangly boy next door had hung around for years, idolising her father whenever he deemed to make an appearance in her life. And slowly her anger at this boy had turned to a puppy love that grew into a giant infatuation scored into her heart. Even when Jake *had* followed in her father's footsteps, becoming another strong, macho construction supervisor, her feelings hadn't changed.

She raised the menu again to hide the rush of emotion, the sorrow, and the grief. The pain was still raw, as if a half-healed wound had been gouged anew by his presence. She should have known better than to trust him in the first place. She should have stuck with hating him—she would have been safe then.

Meg held her breath as she heard the heavy footfalls come closer, felt the rush of air across her bare arm as someone passed by. She could hear him stop, could feel him close. Her throat ached at the irony of meeting Jake here, out of the blue and without warning. What was she going to say to him?

She felt his hand on the menu, tugging it. She held firm.

'*Signorina*, please,' said a deep-accented baritone. 'You eat your minestrone now. I have your order. I take the menu.'

Meg's relief was palpable. She loosened her grip on the menu and it was swept from her hands. Her eyes followed the departing shield as the waiter proceeded to the next table. She wasn't ready for Jake to see her—to come over, to talk to her after years of emptiness.

Her eyes leapt to the neatly arranged table. The cutlery wasn't going to be useful, neither was the vase of flowers, and her soup bowl was out of the question—steaming hot and aromatic.

'Hello, Meg.'

She froze. His voice was unmistakable, low and smooth, awakening her body to long-suppressed reactions. Jake. *Her Jake.* Her heart skipped a beat. She'd thought she'd never hear that voice again. She wasn't sure whether to cry or scream. She looked up.

His eyes bored into hers. Green eyes that tore at her heart. She had the perverse urge to leap into his strong arms and hold him.

Jake stood tall in front of her table, looking tough, his muscles rippling under his cream designer shirt. The years had been kind to him. His features had matured from the smooth and boyish she'd known to the 'seasoned by the world', devilishly handsome face that was now right in front of her.

She sat frozen in her seat. There was too much between them for her to embrace him, too much even to move. He was part of the past and there was no way she'd let him or any other man into her heart again just to break it.

Jake pulled a chair to the table. 'May I?' He carried himself with a new, commanding air of authority. 'You're looking well, Meg.'

She nodded, afraid her voice would betray her if she used it. The scent of his aftershave tormented her with memories of their times together, and hearing her name on his lips was a torture she'd thought she'd never have to endure again.

He turned to Suzie. 'Jacob Adams. I'm Meg's—'

'Friend.' Meg found her voice. 'An old friend.' She gave him a hostile glare. How dared he think he could walk in here and take over? Tell the whole world who he was and what she was to him?

'You don't look that old to me.' Suzie leant her elbows onto the table and rested her chin on her hands. Her friend's hazel eyes glinted and her cherry lips were conspicuously seductive.

Meg squirmed. Suzie was going all out. She had no idea that this guy had no concept of commitment. *She* knew it only too well—she'd learnt it the hard way.

'I'm old enough.' Jake held Suzie's look a moment longer than was necessary. He turned to Meg. 'I hear you're quite a success. I never knew you were going into fashion.'

It was strange to hear him talk so calmly, so familiarly to her, as if there hadn't been an altercation between them at all. She forced her lips to move. 'There was a lot you didn't know about me.'

'You didn't give me a chance.'

'It wasn't like you were planning to stick around to find out anything.' The day she'd found that one-way plane ticket to Delhi had clinched it. It wasn't going to work if he was going to disappear on her again and again, just like her father had.

'You didn't know that.'

'Yes, I did. I knew a lot more than you gave me credit for.'

His eyes darkened. 'I couldn't just walk away from work.'

'You could walk away from me,' she bit out, glaring at him. 'But then I wasn't very high on your list of priorities, was I?'

'You were provided for.' He spoke without a hint of emotion. 'You had everything you could possibly need.'

Not everything, she thought bitterly. Not him. Not the love she needed and deserved. She'd rather go to hell and back than live without love in her life again. She wanted a different life for herself than the one her father had given her. Very different.

'Hey!' Suzie waved her hands between them. 'Truce. What the hell went on between you two?'

'Absolutely nothing.' Meg felt as though her dormant wits had finally returned. She rose from the table. She had nothing to say or prove. Her life was perfect. She didn't need Mr Jacob Adams for anything. 'If you'll excuse me, I'm not hungry any more.'

Jake stood abruptly. 'You can't leave without giving me some answers.'

'Watch me.' Meg sauntered out, holding her breath, fighting against an avalanche of emotion, struggling to hold back the tears that stung behind her eyes.

She wasn't going to let Jacob Adams back into her heart or her life. He'd done enough damage the first time round.

CHAPTER TWO

THE vibrant displays in Meg's shopfront window went unnoticed for the first time. Even her assistants passed in a blur, their voices incoherent as Meg contemplated her conversation with Jake. She was already rehashing it in her mind, wishing she'd said things differently or not at all. If only the waiter had let her keep the menu... But she knew that she couldn't have kept hiding for ever.

She pushed open the door to her private office. The large mahogany desk set against the pastel colours of the walls, the floral cushions adorning the cream sofa and the polished timber floor she had dreamt of for ages now all seemed meaningless. What had he done to her? Usually she found joy and satisfaction in the achievement of her own boutique. She'd struggled against the world, against the odds, and won.

In the space of a couple of minutes Jake's magnetic green eyes had penetrated her carefully constructed world and destroyed her happiness, shattering her contentment. She sank into her chair behind the desk. Why had she gone out to lunch today?

Meg grimaced at Suzie's dedication to shoving her out into the dating scene. Meg hadn't been very co-operative. She'd pushed herself for the last twelve months, trying to break into the exclusive designer world while juggling a hectic private life. Men, although not the last thing on her mind, were an unnecessary complication, an issue she could do without. But Suzie had other plans.

'Meg?' Her secretary, Joyce, tapped on the door and entered. 'Are you all right? You look terrible.'

'I'm fine.' Meg stiffened. 'Lunch just didn't go to plan, that's all.' She fiddled with her pen and tried to avoid Joyce's perceptive eyes. Joyce had been with her almost from the start, but still Meg couldn't bring herself to tell her everything. To tell her the truth about her life.

Joyce pushed her thin-framed glasses up her nose and approached the desk. She dropped a couple of files in front of Meg. 'Did you and Suzie have a falling out?'

Meg wished it was that easy. It was usual for Suzie and she not to see eye to eye on quite a few issues, and Suzie had the awful habit of telling Meg exactly what she thought in the bluntest way. Meg was the first to admit that Suzie was an acquired taste, but Joyce was way off the mark this time.

'You could say that.' Meg bit her lip. Or rather Suzie had been all for falling in while she'd fallen flat. 'I'll call her later.'

'A reporter called and wanted an interview.' Joyce straightened the papers on her desk. 'I said I'd have to check with you.'

Meg sighed and picked up a file. It had had to come, she supposed. Her designs had done well in a fashion show last week, and it was only natural the media and the public were interested in who she was and where she'd come from. Only she wasn't ready to tell. Not yet.

'Can you stall him? I'm so busy at the moment.'

'Are you sure?' Joyce appeared unconvinced. She dithered around the room, dusting the knick-knacks Meg liked to scatter over the shelves.

'Back to the grind,' Meg hinted.

Joyce stopped at the door and patted her coloured hair into place before turning the handle. 'Your one o'clock has arrived early.'

'No worries. Send her in.' Better to get stuck into work than dwell on Jake and her traitorous body. How could he still affect her like that?

'It's a him. By himself.' Joyce closed the door.

A 'him' *was* unusual. She catered for rich women who wanted original outfits for exclusive events. In all the time she'd been in business not one man had come in on his own.

Meg stood up and smoothed down her red top, flicking the creases out of her black trousers. She positioned herself squarely behind her desk, primed to set a good first impression.

The door opened. 'A Mr Jacob Adams,' Joyce announced cheerily, hanging onto the doorhandle whilst admiring the visitor's tall, well-proportioned figure as he walked in.

Meg stared dumbly at Jake.

It wasn't as if her appointment book was empty. He'd either used his charm or his money on Joyce. Or he'd known well in advance where she was and their meeting today at the restaurant had been no accident. Meg tensed. 'Thank you, Joyce,' she said as calmly as she could manage.

Meg glared at Jake. How long had he known where she was? More importantly, how much did he know? Her knees gave out from under her and she disguised her collapse into her high-backed leather chair with as much dignity and grace as she could muster.

The door closed and she leant forward. 'What the blazes are you doing here?' She willed her weakness to vanish so she could come out of her corner fighting. There was no way she was coming out of this second best.

Jake stood there casually, looking as strong and confident on her turf as he would anywhere, she guessed. He carried with him an air of confidence that chafed. His hair seemed a little more ruffled and he'd opened another button on his shirt since lunch, revealing the light scattering of chest hair that she'd used to coil her fingers in.

He strode towards her. 'I want answers.'

'Well, get used to living with disappointment.' She stood up, to feel less intimidated by his height, his breadth, his power. Her legs held.

What gave him the right to come and demand anything? He had chosen what was important to him and it wasn't her. She had gone on without him, managing quite well, on and off. 'What did you do? Bribe my secretary or use your deadly charm on her?'

'Neither.' He shoved his hands into his pockets. 'I did it the old-fashioned way— I made an appointment over the phone three days ago.'

She pressed her lips together and swallowed the rumble of distrust in her belly. It wasn't coincidence that she'd met him at the restaurant. 'You haven't been following me, have you?'

'Your secretary assured me that my appointment fell just *before* your lunch hour, Meg. I had planned to invite you to eat with me, but you'd already gone when I stopped in earlier.'

He probably couldn't stand to wait for her as she'd done for him a million times before. Not just for minutes or hours, but day upon day, month upon month.

Meg shrugged. At least she had something to thank Suzie for—her surprise visits always sent her schedules awry, and today was the perfect day for it. Though maybe it would have been better to have met Jake in private first, rather than in the busy restaurant. At least here she could tell him exactly where to go in the least polite way.

'So I made a few modest enquiries about your movements, and—' He ran his eyes over her. 'You know the rest.'

Meg walked over to her cabinet. She fingered the small, intricate crystal animals—a meditative practice that had always worked before to centre her thoughts. But not today. Not with Jake standing right there in her office, barely two metres away from her. She imagined she could feel the heat of his body radiating from him. She turned to face him. 'I want you to go.'

He covered the distance between them in a moment, his large hands wrapping around her shoulders. 'I've lived long enough without answers, and I'm not leaving your side without them.'

A familiar shiver of awareness coursed through her body and she raised her head to look directly into his face. 'I'll call the police,' she challenged.

His firm mouth pulled tight and his eyes bored into hers with an intensity that jolted her senses. She moistened her dry lips.

'Go ahead. I'm sure they'll be interested to hear that you've dragged them away from real cases just because you're scared of talking to me.'

Meg tried to regain some composure, but she found it difficult even to think straight with his hands branding her arms. 'That's not fair.'

'Life's not fair.' Amusement glinted in his eyes.

'Tell me about it.' It wasn't fair he could still twist her words against her. She bit into her bottom lip fiercely. 'You spoke to Suzie, didn't you?'

'Suzie was very keen to talk about you.'

Her stomach lurched. Suzie had better not have told him everything, or the world would soon be short one gossipmonger. 'And herself, no doubt.'

'Is that jealousy I hear, Megan J?' He watched her intently. 'What's with the J anyway?'

Heat flooded her cheeks. 'J is for James. It's my middle name. Not that you'd remember.' Her father hadn't been able to bear the idea of not using *his* father's name for his only child— a curse when she was young which had finally turned out a blessing when she'd decided to disappear. And it was perfect for her fashion label.

Jake's deep green eyes were dangerously warm. 'Meg, what went wrong?'

The tenderness in his tone shocked her. She looked to her pale ceiling. The wrenching ache in the back of her throat took her by surprise, but she wasn't about to fall into *that* trap. 'If you don't know then you're a bigger idiot than I thought you were.'

'That's unfair.' His grip tightened and his eyes searched hers, as if probing the depths of her soul for answers to questions he couldn't form. 'We were young.'

It was a statement. She didn't need to answer. She didn't want to speak in case she broke the silence.

Meg's ears filled with Jake's sharp, uneven breathing. She looked into his face and the sizzling promise in his eyes scared her.

'And now we're all grown up.' She twisted in his arms and struggled to free herself from his embrace before he did something stupid. 'Can you stick around and face reality?'

He flinched. 'You don't think I know what's real? While you were home I was out working in the real world. Not just tame work in some office. Out in vicious temperatures, remote wild places—it was hard. Harder than you can imagine; harder than you'll ever have to experience.'

She stabbed her finger into his chest. 'You have no idea what I've been through, Jacob Adams, and I don't think you would know real life if you fell over it. What you described isn't real! It sounds like some adventure a Boy Scout would go on—but when he gets home there are people there who need him to stay, not for him to find the next big adventure going.'

'We needed money.' His voice softened. 'I needed to work.' His hands relaxed their grip on her arms and he ran his thumbs gently along her skin.

Her body screamed for all the years of loneliness and neglect. She felt an unwelcome surge of excitement. Making love was the one thing in which they had been in total agreement and unison, and her loins ached at the thought. 'I could have done with less, much less.'

He raked a hand through his dark hair and stared boldly into her eyes.

She held them.

Jake pulled her against his hard body and wrapped her in his warm embrace. She could feel his chin resting against the side of her head, hear him breathing in her perfume, her shampoo, her very essence, and her heart wrenched at the futility of it all.

She pulled back and searched his face.

He was intense, watching her lips.

Meg's heart thudded against her ribs. The vulnerability in his eyes frightened her more than anything else.

He leant towards her and touched her lips with his. The caress was feather-light, sending her stomach into a wild swirl.

His kiss gradually deepened and she surrendered to the sensations running wild in her body. *It was the goodbye kiss they'd never had.*

His mouth moved over hers, devouring its softness, exploring and caressing, and a hunger attacked her. She responded like an animal, wanton and abandoned, and the pain of the past faded in the wake of the passion he was evoking in her.

She had an aching desire to retake what had once been hers, and the need overwhelmed her fears. She plundered his mouth and he responded.

He crushed her to his body.

Time melted away and it was the same as it had been. His lips and hers, dancing in unison. Electricity zinged between them like lightning, their arms and bodies interlocking in an embrace so warm, so hard, so hot that Meg could hardly breathe.

When Jake pulled back he tasted her lips again and again, as though he couldn't get enough of her. Finally, he pulled away.

Her lips were still hungry, as her body was, and it was all she could do to stop herself crying out at his withdrawal.

The corners of Jake's mouth twitched. He seemed to enjoy her struggle to capture her composure. 'It's still there, Meg.'

'It's not enough, Jake,' she managed breathlessly. Her blood pounded wildly through her veins and an aching was aroused in her that she'd kept suppressed for too long. 'I'm going home.' She pulled out of his hold and snatched up her bag. She had to get away from him before she did something stupid.

'Meg.'

His voice cut into her, straight to her core. She stopped.

'You owe me a chance, Meg.'

She spun around. 'What the hell gives you that idea?'

'Damn it, Meg. You're the one who ran away. I want to talk about this.'

'I'm different and you're—you're… You're you! I've grown up.' She looked away to hide the truth. 'I won't live like that again, Jake.' Never again.

She could barely suppress her temper. She wanted to tell him everything she'd been through, all the pain, the hurt, the loneliness, but the words died on her lips. He wasn't any different now from the man she'd known three years ago—it would end just the same. 'I'm not your wife any more.'

CHAPTER THREE

'YOU may not wear my ring any more.' Jake glanced at her bare finger and his gut lurched. 'But we're still married.'

Meg strode resolutely to the door and swung it wide. 'Goodbye, Mr Adams.' She lifted her chin in defiance.

Jake ignored the door.

She was still beautiful. Her large blue eyes and lush red lips spoke directly to his body. The spark in her voice fired his passion and her ivory skin called to him to touch her again and again.

Meg needed someone looking out for her. It could have been him if he hadn't been blinded by work. He should've seen she wasn't happy. Her leaving him like that had been confirmation of his greatest fear.

Marrying her had been right for him, but not for her. He'd taken advantage of her youth, her naivety, and paid for it with a gaping hole in his life.

But now he was back. He was worthy of her now. He had money, security, and was hell-bent on not making the same mistakes again. He was sure that, whatever her reason for leaving, he could make it right now.

Jake could barely restrain his need to make her his again. But he knew from Meg's chilly reception that she wasn't ready to let them pick up where they left off. She wasn't even willing to see how much he'd changed. *If only he knew why.* Then he'd have some chance of sorting this all out.

A muscle quivered in his jaw. 'I mean it, Meg. I'm not leaving your side until you tell me what happened.'

Meg crossed her arms over her soft, full breasts, her lips pressed together in a grim line.

The look on her face said it all. Jake knew it well. Hers was a look of defiance, as if she'd rather be struck dead than give in to him. He'd spent enough years coercing men to work to know he had to change tack or lose.

'Let me start over, Meg. This has gotten all out of proportion. I came to find you so I could work out what went wrong. So…' He paused, faltering in his course of action. She had to feel safe, see him differently. 'So I don't make the same mistakes with…' His befuddled mind dredged up the name of the woman who had handled his company's business logo and card designs. 'With Vivian.'

Meg's arms dropped to her sides. Her lips parted in surprise, her whole jaw slack, blank eyes staring at him.

Of all the rotten… Meg's mind ran through a dozen expletives. The nerve! Coming to ask her to explain to him what he'd done wrong so he didn't wreck his precious relationship with this Vivian. The only reason!

She clenched her hands by her sides. No wonder it had taken him so long to find her. He'd been waiting for a good reason. And her name was Vivian.

She walked stiffly back to her desk, moving around the expanse of timber, hoping for some barrier between them. This had had to come.

She had known that it would eventually. Though she'd expected some document in the mail from his solicitor, demanding she sign divorce papers so he could marry some name-less, faceless woman. Not *him* in person. 'I guess you'll want a divorce, then.' She ground the words out from between her teeth.

He looked taken aback for a moment. 'Yes, of course. But I'm not going to sign anything until I understand fully what went wrong with us.' He seated himself casually in one of her embroidered chairs and propped a foot up on his knee, exuding a calm that Meg wished she could find herself.

'Then why the hell did you kiss me?' She leant heavily on the desk, wishing she could spit fire and strike him down where he sat, with her eyes alone.

He shrugged matter-of-factly. 'Habit. Sorry. Forgot who you were for a moment— I just got carried away with your lips so close, beg-ging to be taken.'

'They were not begging!' She turned away, willing her cheeks to cool. She'd been acting like a total idiot. She mentally rehashed their conversation and kicked herself. He'd been harping on about wanting to know what had happened in the past, not inviting himself into her life, or her future. She took several big breaths to slow her pounding heart. Here she was trying to convince him that she was mature now and she'd been rambling like a scared child.

She managed a smile, taking her eyes off his powerful body and staring at the fabric samples on her desk. 'I'll be glad to discuss your failings as a husband.' Meg revelled in the idea of doling out a serving of revenge. She gritted her teeth. She would love to bring him down a peg or two with some hard truths. 'Let's say dinner tonight at seven, at Vivo's?'

'Same place as lunchtime?' He hesitated. 'Okay, sure.' He rose in one fluid motion.

'And bring Vivian,' Meg added, inspired. She couldn't get into any trouble with Jake if his precious girlfriend was there. And it would be darned interesting to see whom he was making such a fuss over. Then she could put a face to the woman who could tolerate Jake's lack of commitment.

'Vivian?'

'Yes. Bring along the woman you want to spend the rest of your life with.' Her stomach twisted into a painful knot at the thought. 'She's the one who'd be most interested to hear what I have to say. She did come with you, didn't she?' Meg raised an eyebrow and held her breath. Maybe this woman was involved with him for his money and his body, not for love.

'She's in Brisbane.' Jake's voice faded, losing its strength. 'Won't be down until... tomorrow afternoon.' He stopped and drew a deep breath. 'That's what I came in here about, actually. I wanted to check out the place for her. She wants a gown for some charity ball on the Gold Coast.'

'Two birds with one stone?'

He shifted his weight and thrust his hands into his pockets. 'Yeah, something like that.'

'And do I check out?' Meg didn't know what to think any more. Her head felt as though it would split in half with the strain of the day's turn of events. 'Of course I won't let on that you kissed me. I wouldn't want to upset the apple cart.' Or did she? Certainly she had some duty to let the woman know what she was getting into with Jake—she'd just have to find a way to wend his womanising ways into the conversation.

'Thanks, I appreciate it.'

'No worries.' She smiled. 'Now, if you don't mind, I've got work to do.' Like plotting revenge, or collapsing in a heap, or both.

'Will you still come tonight?' Jake moved towards the door with all the satisfaction of a beast that had captured its prey.

'Sure.' A meal with Jake couldn't hurt, and finding out all about Vivian and making a meal of her would be exactly what her ego needed to repair some of the damage.

'Vivian?' Jake could almost picture her behind her desk, ebony-black hair coiled on top of her head, pristine suit, sharp eyes and pinched mouth. Nothing like Meg.

'Yes.'

He gripped the phone tighter. 'Jacob Adams, JAKCO Constructions. You may not remember me. We met at the golf club, you did some work for me...?'

'Of course I do,' she purred. 'Jacob, how are you? How's work going? How's the logo? The business cards? Is my ad in the *Yellow Pages* working?'

He swallowed. He hadn't needed one in the first place; he got his work from tenders out of the newspapers mostly. But he hadn't been able to bring himself to disappoint the efficient woman. 'Works great.'

'Good.' There was silence. 'What can I do for you, then?'

He dragged air into his lungs, stewing on how to phrase his request. 'I need your services for a week, in Melbourne. Strictly business, of course.'

'Of course. Sounds intriguing, tell me more.'

What could he possibly say? He wasn't about to blurt out the truth to a stranger. 'I

need a companion to avoid any misinterpreta-
tion of my actions—'

'Does this involve a woman?'

'Yes.'

'And you don't want her to get the wrong
idea. I'm assuming you'll pay for my ex-
penses, my time away from work...?'

'Of course.'

'My company could bear closing its doors
for the right price,' she tittered.

Jake quoted a figure he was sure would fully
compensate her for any loss of business.
Money wasn't an issue. Only Meg was, and it
was blatantly obvious she felt threatened by
him. If he could get her to let her guard
down...

'Are you offering anything extra?'

He racked his brain as to what more she
could want. 'Yes. You get a dress by a designer in Melbourne.' Women loved clothes.
He smiled. He should have the deal sewn up.

'Not exactly what I was expecting, but why
not? When do I start?'

Jake couldn't help but smile as he dropped the phone into its cradle. That was one problem solved. Now he could focus *all* his energies in one direction only...

Meg hadn't counted on the noisy, cluttered restaurant of lunch turning into such a romantic venue at night. The lights were dimmed, candles were lit on each cloth-covered table, and there was soft music. Couples nestled everywhere, leaning close and enjoying the atmosphere.

She held her hands together tightly, kneading them as she approached the tall figure at the bar. He wore a cream cotton shirt and dark Armani trousers, but she knew better than anyone that clothes didn't make the man. So he dressed well, and exuded a subtle scent of cologne that invaded her nostrils and sent goosebumps all over her skin... She felt like standing there for a while and just drinking in the sight of him, but she'd tortured herself enough for one day. 'Jake.'

He turned, his eyes running down over her, from her black silk blouse to her black loose-fitting trousers and high-heeled boots. 'Meg. I was starting to think you weren't coming.' His smile widened in approval.

Her stomach fluttered and she was glad she'd resisted the urge to dress to the hilt. Although some part of her wanted to rub his face in what he'd missed out on, the other part was more than content for him to go his way with this Vivian woman and leave her and hers well enough alone. What she needed was love, and Jake wasn't the one to give her that. Jake was a load she wasn't willing to bear again. 'I got caught up at home.'

His eyebrows drew together in a frown. 'Are you involved with anyone?'

'That's none of your business.'

Jake cast her a quick glance. 'I'm sure the guy would be interested to know you're still married.' He paused, but she didn't respond. 'Did you tell him you were going out with your husband?' Jake clenched his fists. 'He could have come too, you know.'

'Let's get a table, shall we?' Meg didn't want to get into the details of her personal life with Jake. She wasn't about to blurt out what she'd gone through in the last three years, or who was waiting for her at home.

'Fine.' Jake raised a hand and signalled one of the Italian waiters. They sat down at a much-too-quiet table in a corner. Jake ordered wine and they both ordered their meal. Then he turned to her.

'So, tell me what happened to us.'

'Now?' She lowered her eyes and moved uneasily in her seat. He had never been one for patience or subtlety, but she'd expected to have a chance at indigestion before she tackled that one.

'Good a time as any.' Jake leant on the table, reducing the space between them by precious inches. His boldly handsome face smiled warmly at her.

Meg felt her stomach curl. She'd rehearsed her story all afternoon, but it seemed to stick in her throat. She took a gulp of water from her glass. It was one thing lamenting Jake's actions for years, another to tell him to his face how he'd broken her heart.

The wine arrived, and Meg snatched up the goblet and gulped the deep red vintage. It went down quickly, hitting her stomach with such force that Meg slapped the glass down to cover the unpleasant response. She hadn't eaten lunch—hadn't eaten anything since breakfast, figuring her poor belly was suffering enough with stress without adding food to it.

'That good, hey?' Jake teased, his wide smile sending her senses into a spin.

'I'm sorry. I don't know where to start.' Her mind reeled with confusion. Where was the level-headed woman she knew so well? The one who'd coped despite all the obstacles, trials and tribulations sent her way? She had the perverse urge to run home to see if she'd left her lying out on the bed, where her clothes had been all afternoon, taunting her with what was coming.

'Tell me anything, then. Tell me about your career.'

She was glad of the reprieve, though cautious at what he was up to with this show of civility. Meg rattled on for what seemed like ages, carefully choosing her words so she didn't trip herself into revealing more than she wanted to. She told him lightly about how she'd eked out a meagre existence above a garage in Toorak, her main patron being her landlady, who'd believed so much in her designs that she'd advertised by word of mouth.

Meg didn't want to harp on any of the details. It wouldn't do her any good to fuel any sense of guilt Jake might have for what had happened in the past. If he knew what she'd been through, and how much she owed, she hated to think what he might do; his over-inflated sense of duty might run rampant, all over her well-ordered life. And the way his eyes never left her face while she talked, the way his hands gripped the edge of the table, suggested he wasn't as calm as he was pretending to be.

'Your landlady sounds like Winnie.'

'Yes,' Meg answered.

'You miss her?'

'Yes.' Her father's aunt, Winnie, had died just after Meg had begun college. She hadn't been like a mother to her—she'd never known a mother. But Winnie had been like a very old big sister. She'd been her friend more than anything, and not afraid to tell her anything that she'd needed to know—although sometimes Meg felt she'd given Winnie more of an education about life than her great-aunt had given her.

Mostly she remembered the fairytales Winnie had told her as a child, of the princess being saved by the handsome prince, and how she was carried off to the castle in the air. Later, when Winnie's eyesight had started to fail her, Meg would read *her* stories. She was glad that she'd died peacefully in her sleep; it gave her the hope that her old friend had been dreaming of her own prince when she'd left.

It had been a shock finding her there like that. And of course Dad hadn't been there. She'd been alone. She'd had to work out all the details herself while Dad wired her the money. He hadn't even made it to the funeral. But he'd made it to his own, only a year later.

'How is your mother?' Meg asked politely. Jake's mother, Moira, had never liked her. She'd gone out of her way to make sure Meg knew how disappointed she was at Jake's decision to marry her. Moira had looked daggers at Meg at the wedding, had ignored her totally at the reception, and had made herself conspicuously absent when Jake and Meg moved to a home of their very own.

'She's fine.'

'Any more stepfathers?'

Jake shot her a dark look. 'No.'

'I'm sorry, that was out of line.' Moira had gone through three husbands and several lovers. Meg was sure it was her personality that attracted them; she tended to be light and cheerful most of the time. It was the rest of the time that was the problem.

Their meal arrived and Meg tried to concentrate on the flavour of her lasagna, but its taste was lost on her. Nothing registered with her as real except Jake on the other side of the table and the strained distance between them.

What did she care anyway? That was the point, after all, she kept telling herself. All she had to do was get this over and done with and she could get back to her life. The thought echoed around in her mind. *It had a hollow ring to it.*

'And how's Danny?' Meg was sure that he was a safe subject, if not a flamboyant one. Danny had been Jake's best friend for as long as she could remember, sticking with him through thick and thin despite their different natures.

She could see Jake swallow hard. 'Haven't seen him in years.' The indifference in his icy tone shook her. They'd been so close. She would have thought nothing could come between the two of them; they were inseparable. The times Danny would drag Jake off to the pub or to a party…

She shook herself. 'So how's work?' She knew that would get a response. For Jake there was nothing more important. She swallowed another mouthful of lasagna and felt it struggle down her throat.

'Do you really care, or are you just humouring me?'

'Of course I'm interested to hear what adventures you've found yourself over the last three years.' She felt she needed reminding of what had held a higher priority than she had, so she could crush the flutters coming from the vicinity of her heart.

Jake raised an eyebrow. 'As you know I went to Delhi. That was for a gas pipeline. The job dragged on and when I got back you were gone. Well and truly gone.'

She could hear the bitterness in his voice and concentrated on her plate. She swallowed the brick in her throat. 'Go on.'

He explained how he'd gone from one construction site to another, until it had all blurred into one conglomerate called work. The way Jake spoke it seemed the passion he'd once had for his work was missing. Either that or he was unwilling to share it with her. She didn't blame him if that was the case.

Jake put down his spoon, his half-eaten *gelato* melting in the bowl. 'So what happened, Meg?'

She took a big breath. 'I didn't want to be left alone, Jake. My father had done it long enough. I couldn't do it again.'

'That's it?'

'It was enough,' Meg whispered hoarsely, her voice threatening to abandon her completely. She wanted to scream at him that he had no idea what it was like to be alone, to wait and then finally, when you thought you'd get some attention and love, something better came up—and it was back to the waiting. And waiting was rejection all over again. Hovering around the front window, the phone and the mailbox for any word from him.

'Look, I don't know whether I ever actually said it, but I'm sorry about your dad. I loved him too.' Jake reached a hand over the table, enclosing hers in his warmth.

A delicious shudder heated Meg's body. She looked up and her heart lurched madly at the heart-rending tenderness of his gaze.

'I know.' She put down the wine. 'It must have been hard for you to be there—' She choked on the words. She knew only too well now what had gone on in the last few minutes of her father's life.

'I'll never forget that moment.' Jake faltered. 'When that chain slipped and that pipe fell...I'll never forget.'

Tears sprang into her eyes and she wiped them away jerkily. That moment had changed her whole life. If Jake hadn't been there; if her father had been standing a metre to one side; if she'd seen the truth before she'd married Jake...

She didn't dare look at Jake. She couldn't, just in case she broke down and told him everything—opening herself up again to him and paying for it later.

The silence between them hung heavily, becoming harder and harder to penetrate as the minutes ticked by. Meg's mind fumbled for something to say. Anything to say.

'So when is Vivian arriving?' she blurted.

Jake snapped his eyes to hers, then fixed them on the bill on the table. 'Oh, um…at six…tomorrow evening.' He dropped some notes onto the bill and stood up.

'I'll make an appointment for her on Friday, then.' Meg rose, wrapping her black cardigan around her shoulders. Pain squeezed her heart at how easily she'd been replaced in his life— if she'd ever been a part of it at all.

He put a hand around her shoulder, letting it drop to the small of her back as he steered her out of the restaurant.

The touch of his hand was almost unbearable in its gentleness, reminding her again of all she'd lost.

'I'll take you home.'

'No!' The last thing she wanted was Jake anywhere near her house. 'I'm fine. I don't live far. A taxi is fine.'

'If it's not far, then there's no argument.' His voice was firm, final, and he showed no sign of relenting as he nudged her towards the parked cars.

They walked down the footpath and Meg's mind rattled around in circles. Mixed feelings surged through her. Half of her wanted to heave the hard truth from her shoulders onto his; the other wanted nothing more than to crawl into her bed and wait until he was gone again.

Jake stopped beside a black BMW.

Meg was surprised. 'No four-wheel drive?'

'I'm not your father, Meg.' His expression darkened with an unreadable emotion.

Meg looked away. She knew that! Every inch of her knew that. How was she going to survive the drive with him when already the tension between them was making her ill?

He opened the door for her and she slipped into the car. The heady new leather smell hit her first, and then the opulence of what appeared to be a brand-new car. The seat cushioned her perfectly, and the dashboard was a myriad of controls that blurred into insignificance as Jake claimed the driver's seat beside her.

The spacious car suddenly felt cramped. The leather scent mingled with the scent of his spicy cologne, igniting Meg's senses, reminding her body of what it had once known, what was so close to her again.

She breathed slowly, willing herself to keep her attention away from him, away from his muscled thighs so close to her. The fabric of his trousers stretched taut as he worked the clutch, gunning the motor to life and slipping the car into motion. One hand held the wheel, the other was on the stick shift...large hands and long fingers that Meg recalled being as gentle and persuasive as they were hard and strong.

The journey seemed to take for ever. When he finally pulled up outside the terraced house she couldn't help but expel her breath in relief.

'My driving that bad, is it?'

'I'm sorry.' She could feel the heat rise in her cheeks. He must think her an idiot. 'Not used to it, I guess.' Better to let him think he was a crazed driver than for him to know how much her body longed for him.

Jake cast a long look over his shoulder and ahead, down the dimly lit, deserted street, and then at her home. 'I'll walk you to your door.'

'Thanks, but I'm fine. I can get to my own door without help.' She could see there was a light on through the lacy curtains of the front windows. The outside light shone onto the intricate paintwork she'd had done to bring the worn old masterpiece back to her former glory. The house was brick but all the trims were timber, now a glorious rich cream.

'A gentleman wouldn't have a lady go to her door alone in the dark.'

'What gentleman?' she scoffed, trying to lighten the mood between them. 'I don't see one.' She looked around the pristine car, and outside, up and down the quiet street, wishing fervently that Jake would just let it go and drive away.

'You're not looking,' he said in what sounded like all seriousness, and he alighted from the car before she could say anything else.

'Oh, really?' she called after him. She dug her nails into the soft leather of her handbag as Jake opened her door. 'I *can* do it myself.'

'I have no doubt of that. But I'd like to show you how my manners have improved.' He held out his hand to her.

Meg eyed it suspiciously before surrendering hers to him. She felt the surge of blood from her fingertips to her toes—he was radiating his charm and she had to be mindful not to succumb again.

He released her and cupped his hand gently under her elbow, steering her up the shadowy path to her door.

His touch was torture; her traitorous body responded instantly with shivers down her back. 'I'm sure Vivian is thrilled with your manners.' Meg needed to remind him as well as herself where his loyalties lay to still her body's frenzy.

Jake didn't falter.

Meg crossed her fingers. Nearly there. Her heart beat faster with every step closer to her front door. She wanted desperately for him to go, to turn around right there and speed off in his car, without looking back and definitely without going any closer. But she knew it was useless. Any more argument or protest would make him suspicious.

Meg extracted her elbow from his touch as soon as she reached the doorstep. She fumbled for her keys in her bag, cursing them under her breath for being so elusive at a time like this.

'Well, thanks for a lovely evening. I hope you didn't mind me being honest with you.' She hoped she sounded calm and composed.

'Not at all. Though I sort of expected a bit more.' He regarded her with a speculative glance. 'Is there something you're not telling me?'

A cry from inside made Meg cringe.

'What was that?' There was an edge of concern in his voice. He tilted his head and looked at her uncertainly.

'A cat?' Meg prayed he'd accept it and leave.

'There's no way that sounded like a cat.' She could see his jaw clench in the soft light, and his eyes narrowed and bored into hers as if he could hunt for an answer in her face.

The cry sounded again, more urgent, curling Meg's stomach into knots. 'I share the place with a girl with a baby,' she blurted. She shoved the key into the lock and turned it.

'Meg?' Jake said hesitantly.

She paused, turning to him. 'Yes?' she asked innocently.

The door flung wide. The young girl's eyes were wide and full of concern, the toddler on her hip reaching out. 'Thank God you're back. He's been crying for you for ages. He just won't settle.' She thrust the little boy into Meg's arms, ignoring Jake next to her.

'Mama,' the toddler cried. He wrapped his small arms tightly around Meg and buried his face in her neck.

Meg couldn't bring herself to look at Jake. What could she possibly say?

CHAPTER FOUR

JAKE'S mind whirled at a sickening speed. Meg so tense, making excuses…a child…this baby boy…Meg a mum… Every drop of blood seeped to the pit of his stomach.

A wild giddiness attacked him. *His* baby…?

He clenched his hands and tried to still the onslaught of feelings flailing around inside him. He had to think clearly, rationally, not jump to any rash assumptions.

Logic always helped him through his difficulties at work, had always worked before—there was no reason for it not to work now.

He raked his hair with his hands and eyed Meg warily. She wouldn't have left him if she was pregnant. She wasn't like that. Surely to God she would have told him if she was pregnant with his baby, would have known he would never turn his back on her. *If* he was his.

'Meg.' His voice was barely a whisper.

She stiffened as though he'd struck her.

'I've got to get going.' The sitter grabbed a cardigan off a chair by the door, appearing oblivious to the bombshell she'd dropped.

Meg seemed to suddenly register the young woman. She turned to her and shifted the little boy to her hip. 'Thanks. Ring you later. About tomorrow.'

Jake barely noticed the girl step past him. He forced air into his lungs. All he could do was stare at the little bundle of human being wrapped in Meg's arms and at the woman he'd wronged. So badly.

He should have spent more time around kids. He could do the maths in his head if only he knew how old this baby was.

One thing was for sure. She wouldn't have had time to meet another guy, have a nine-month pregnancy, then a baby this sort of size and a business all in the time they'd been apart. He clamped down on the hot fist of pain in his gut. She couldn't have!

Meg stepped into the hallway. The light reflected well off the high ceilings and the ornate plasterwork, lighting up Meg's face. She was tense, almost harrowed, her brow creased and her eyes wide.

The ache was unbearable. He wanted to take her in his arms and hold her, kiss away her fears. He could make it right. He had to. 'Where're you going?' His voice erupted too sharply, too demanding.

Her head snapped around. 'Inside.' The baby made a gurgling noise, his tiny chubby fingers gripping her tighter. Meg straightened and glared at him. 'I don't consider standing on the doorstep a long-term activity.'

Jake raised his hand, reaching out to her as she turned her back to him. 'Meg?' he pleaded. Couldn't she see what this was doing to him?

She finally turned, halfway down the hallway. 'You'd better come in for coffee, then.'

'Something stronger may be a good idea.' He tried to joke. Anything to wipe that pained expression off her face; anything to see her smile.

She glared at him. 'I don't keep anything stronger in the house. You could go to the pub.'

And not come back. The unspoken insinuation hit him in the chest with a disquieting resonance. He covered his response by striding into the entrance and closing the door firmly behind him. He was going to get answers. Here and now.

'Meg?' He sounded like a broken record and hated himself for it. 'How old is he?'

'Nearly two.' Her voice shook.

His heart skittered. Why was she so upset? Surely she knew he'd love her to have had his baby? Unless…his best mate Danny had been doing a lot more than just looking out for her while he was away…

Cold fury squeezed his heart. The gaping emptiness seemed as if it would swallow him, just as it had done when he'd found Meg gone.

'Is he—?' He swallowed hard, the words refusing to form. 'Is the boy—?'

'Of course he is,' Meg bit out. 'If you took a minute and really looked at him you'd see his eyes, his chin…'

'But, Meg...' His voice wavered. He sucked in a deep breath. *Get a grip, man.* 'Why?'

'What did you expect?' Her tone was harsh, husky, deep. 'You were never there!'

Jake turned away, bile rising in his throat. Danny was the reason she'd run off! Meg hadn't been able to stand the shame of falling pregnant to Dan and had left him. And it was his fault. He'd practically forced them on each other.

He clenched his fist and eyed the wall. He needed to punch something badly. If he'd been around, if he'd listened, maybe they could've worked it out...worked something out so she didn't have to leave.

He held himself rigid. He was in control. He'd lived his whole life vowing to live up to his responsibilities, promising himself no child would suffer as he'd suffered, without a father, without a sense of security.

'Meg,' he said softly, turning. How could he make it up to her? What had she been through the last couple of years, keeping the sordid truth from him? He watched her as she shifted the child on her hip and slipped out of the room without looking at him.

She'd slept with another man; the truth echoed in his mind, taunting him. Anger churned in his belly, rising up until he felt he would explode.

Jake moved into the hall and stared at the stairs as if they were some impenetrable barrier. He was a stranger here, a stranger to her life and a stranger to her baby. He dug his nails into his palms. He'd certainly mucked it up.

If only he'd sat down and thought everything through before he'd come tearing down here. If only he'd thought before he'd swept her off her feet three years ago. If only he'd had more control. But he hadn't seen past his own desire. He'd wanted her, wanted her so badly. He just hadn't stopped to think what she wanted, what was best for her. He'd wanted to think that *he* was the best thing for her.

Jake could hear her moving around upstairs, a muffled sobbing clawing at his ears and his heart. He was a bloody jerk. He didn't deserve anything from Meg except a punch in the face.

He'd left her to the likes of Danny and messed her life up. Some help that was to her! She was better off without him!

Meg finally returned. Jake searched her face but he couldn't see anything past the cool mask she wore. It had to be true. She couldn't even look at him. No wonder she hadn't wanted him around—he was a constant reminder of the past.

His misery was like a steel weight. 'I'll bring the divorce papers over on Friday,' Jake blurted. The words tasted like bile.

He saw her freeze, stiffen, then turn. 'Sure.' The faint smile she cast him held a touch of sadness that tore at his heart.

It wasn't meant to be like this. He'd thought he had it all worked out, everything planned— but he hadn't accounted for a child. The little guy changed everything.

Vivian and her supposed dress came to him through the fog. He'd talked her into flying down to get a dress made by Megan J. He'd paid her to come down and play in this charade, rearrange her schedule for him—he wasn't going to ruin things for her too. 'Is it still okay for Vivian—?'

'No worries.' Meg didn't meet Jake's gaze as she moved past him. She didn't want him to see she'd been crying. A divorce. She'd known it was coming from the moment he mentioned that Vivian woman. But this? Now? His cold words chilled her heart.

She was a fool. Despite all he'd done to her, she still cared what he thought of her. And now he truly hated her for keeping his son from him.

'Do you want a cuppa?' It was the least she could do, and would maybe give her a chance to justify her actions.

'No, I've outstayed my welcome.' He moved down the hallway hurriedly, as if another minute in her sordid company would make him retch. 'I'll leave you in peace.'

He was at the front gate by the time she reached the front door, still ajar. 'I named him Tommy.' It hurt that he hadn't stopped to ask, didn't care about their son at all. But what could she expect when she'd kept him secret for so long?

It was no excuse that she hadn't known about the baby until well after she'd run. She'd suspected for the first month that it was a stress thing, but when the morning sickness had assailed her in the second month she had had to accept the truth. That she was still alone, that everything Jake's mother and Danny had said was true—her life with Jake had been a lie. And she was pregnant with his child.

Jake paused for a moment and stiffened, but he didn't turn.

Meg wanted to scream at him. Wanted to accuse him of all the things his mother had told her about, all the betrayals with other women. She wanted to charge him with the abominable truth his best mate Danny had revealed, wanted desperately for her guilt to be absolved. But the words wouldn't come, only the tears.

Jacob Adams disappeared into the night.

CHAPTER FIVE

MEG wasn't sure whether she wanted Friday to come quickly or slowly. At times the minutes dragged by, torturing her with flashbacks of her interactions with Jake, her stupid responses, and a barrage of possible witty comebacks that now lay dead on her tongue— unused and useless. Other times the hours flew by, giving her little time to prepare for the interaction to come. The nights were the worst, when her mind would torture her with a past that held so many good memories, and so many bad ones.

Meg closed her eyes, refusing to dwell on how the news of his son would affect Jake. There was little chance he'd leave her life alone now, and the constant fear he might fight for Tommy wasn't entirely out of the question. Look what she'd denied him.

It was a relief that he knew in some ways, and a surprise to see that something could dent Jake's armour. She'd come up against that armour enough times to know it well. Now, years later, she'd guessed why it was so formidable. All the men going through his mother's door had prompted him to don his suit of protective armour at will, to isolate him from getting attached to any of them, from feeling angry or betrayed about the flippant way his mother discarded them, one by one. The trouble was, nothing else got through to him.

Jake hadn't called or come by or left any messages with Joyce for her, and it worried Meg. He was either up to something or didn't care. Either way, she didn't like it.

Old fears and uncertainties swamped her. She had the urge to run away and hide, but she couldn't ignore him now. He wasn't thousands of kilometres away; he had come looking for her. Albeit later than she'd wished, by about two and a half years. But he was here now, and it was time to deal with it.

Meg pulled her hairbrush from the drawer of her desk and dragged it fiercely through her hair, taming the wild short cut to its chic potential, ignoring the pain. She was sure it was nothing to what she was going to endure today.

The phone shattered her reverie.

'Megan, Mrs Bolton is on the phone. She sounds quite flustered,' Joyce explained. 'Shall I put her through?'

'Yes, of course.' Meg hit the button on her phone. 'Mrs Bolton. How are you?'

She'd been very lucky to find out about the loft above Mrs Bolton's garage being available, through an old school mate who'd also done design at college. She'd lived and worked there for a long while, and the old lady had turned out to be her greatest help and support. Meg didn't know what would have happened to her and Tommy without her. 'What can I do for you?'

'Oh, Meg, dear. I have some terrible news.' Mrs Bolton's voice creaked as she spoke. 'I don't know how to tell you, how to ask.'

'Just tell me,' Meg said firmly. Nothing the lovely old woman could tell her could be half so terrible as what she'd gone through the last few days.

'I'm sorry, dear.' She spoke quietly. 'I seem to have messed up my finances. My accountant—he's my brother's son, you know—he's concerned and has asked me to talk to you about...' She paused, struggling for a word, no doubt. She did it quite often, dithering about until the little librarian in her head tossed half a dozen books around before finding the dictionary.

Meg waited patiently, an unpleasant uneasiness brewing in her stomach. What could Mrs Bolton's nephew possibly want from her? She'd been faithfully paying off the low-interest loan her patron had given her from day one.

'Refinancing. Yes, he told me to ask you to refinance.' She tsked a little, patronisingly. 'That boy is always overreacting. I'm sure I'll manage, Meg.'

Meg's stomach fell to the floor. She had a contract with Mrs Bolton, but there was no way she could refuse and see the old woman suffer for her faith in Meg as a designer. She was the only person who'd supported her while she was pregnant and scratching out her designs, struggling to make a living from the occasional dress she'd managed to sell through consignment at a local boutique. Mrs Bolton was the one who'd made her own place possible.

'It's no problem at all, Mrs Bolton,' Meg lied. 'I'll talk to a bank manager first thing on Monday about it.'

'Are you sure, dear? He said you don't have to, but to ask you if you could.'

Meg rang off, reassuring her dear friend that it was no trouble at all. Meg would just have to find the money elsewhere. Whatever it took.

Fear knotted inside her. The lifestyle she had would be gone. She'd have to put in serious hours to secure enough income to make the bank payments, plus wages and costs. The thought tore at her heart. She'd always had time to give Tommy fair access to his mother. Now it was going to be different—unless she gave up her boutique and scaled down again.

Panic, like she'd known three years ago, welled in her throat. Her perfect life was falling to pieces.

She stared at her door. There was no point upsetting everyone else with the news. Her girls didn't need to worry too—not until she found out exactly what the bank's attitude was. She'd keep this to herself—and especially from Jake.

The knock on her door startled her. She wasn't ready.

Meg smoothed down the creases in her trousers with rapid jerky slaps and stood up. 'Come in.' She kicked herself for sounding so wimpy. This was it. The time had come. She'd asked for it and now she'd got it—the love of Jake's life in her boutique.

'Come in,' she yelled, with all the strength she could muster. She stood tall and straight, throwing out her chest and sucking in her stomach.

Joyce opened the door and a tall, curvaceous woman slithered into her office, dressed in a blue body suit that looked more painted on than she did poured in. Jake Adams followed close behind.

Heat rushed under Meg's skin. She watched his strong, masculine body saunter into the room. His taste in clothes was impeccably simple. A cream polo shirt and blue jeans adorned what Meg secretly thought was perfection, and his tanned muscular arms taunted her with memories of their warmth, their protection, as they'd used to wrap around her.

Her gaze locked to his. He watched her from under his dark lashes, arms folded, his expression unreadable as he leant against the bookshelf. His slow perusal of her made her distinctly aware of her own appearance. She tore her eyes away—she couldn't bear to watch his reaction.

She didn't hold a candle to the new woman in Jake's life. Although Meg's cream trouser suit and chemise were stylish they couldn't compete with the package the blue suit came in—a good four inches taller, a great deal more exotic-looking, and built on a much less substantial frame than she was. If she could have guessed Vivian's profession she would have guessed a model.

'Ms Shelton,' Joyce announced with a flourish. She straightened her glasses on her nose. 'And Mr Adams—again.' Joyce turned on her heel and left.

Meg watched Vivian cast an unreadable look at Jake. What it conveyed didn't seem to reach him. His impassive features remained the same. Just how close were they?

'I'm so pleased to meet you, Ms James.' Vivian held out a dainty hand in that limp-wristed fashion that so many pretentious social climbers affected. Her facial bones were delicately carved, her mouth full, her hair jet-black, her manner haughty. 'I can't wait to see what you make for me.'

'Me too.' Meg cast a long look at Jake, who remained rigid and silent. She could imagine Vivian Shelton in a spider suit, complete with pincers and web. How had Jake ended up with *her*? He was certainly travelling in different circles from those of three years ago. It had all been mates' parties and pubs back then, with plenty of beer and games. It seemed as if Jake had finally decided to grow up after she'd left, and his tastes had matured alongside.

'I've been watching your career.' Vivian swept around the office, running her hands over the soft fabric sofa, over the glass shelves of the cabinets and over the little knick-knacks. 'I just loved your designs for the Melbourne races.'

It was hard to keep focused on Vivian when Meg's eyes kept returning to Jake. Why had he come if he was just going to stand there and stare stonily into the distance?

'So shall we start?' Vivian asked stiffly.

Meg shook herself. The woman couldn't be blind to Meg ogling the man in her life as if he was on the menu. 'Yes. Of course.'

She walked over to her desk and picked up her drawing pad and pencils, suppressing the blood that was running to her cheeks. 'You may find this boring, Jake. I'd suggest you come back for Ms Shelton in an hour.'

'Fine.' He straightened, swung open the door and stepped out.

Meg flushed. She looked the other way and breathed. Not a word about Tommy. She closed her eyes, the bitter cold ache of despair washing over her. Of course he wasn't about to talk about his son in front of his future wife. Meg pressed her fingers to her temples to try and stave off the headache she felt coming on.

As the door closed the walls seemed to close in on Meg. Her breath came in ragged gasps as she eyed Vivian Shelton. All her bold intentions had dissolved in Jake's wake. There was nothing to say to this woman, nothing at all for Meg to discuss, no reason for her to be in the room with her save for a dress.

Her throat tightened, her mind screaming unuttered shouts of protest—she wasn't up to this. Meg almost stumbled to the door in her rush to escape, holding up a finger as casually as she could. 'Just one minute, Ms Shelton.'

Meg swung open the door and stepped right into Jake.

She yanked the door shut behind her.

His skin was warm, as was the scent of him, filling her with images of things they'd once done with each other, once known about each other. Like how Jake loved chocolate frogs, poached eggs, black coffee and making love in the morning. And how she'd loved the feel of him against her, his strong muscles beneath her hands, the touch of his soft lips and narrow hips, and how he'd loved her to wrap her legs around him.

'What—?' He turned and searched her eyes.

She didn't know what he saw, but his eyes softened. 'I—I want...' Her mind was a haze of memory and her body was drowning in sensation. 'I wanted to ask you how much she knows—*if* she knows about us, that we're—' She couldn't even say married.

'No. She doesn't know anything—*yet*.' He shifted his weight onto his heels, shoving his hands into pockets. 'I'd appreciate it if you don't say anything personal to her.'

'No worries.' Meg's voice was hoarse with frustration. She'd given him the opportunity to talk to her without that woman, and still he said nothing about their son. Her throat ached in defeat. 'Okay.'

Jake's eyes raked over her boldly, his eyes clouded, his face guarded.

Meg grabbed the door handle, intent on leaving his disturbing presence. How had she messed up her life so badly? She'd had the perfect boy next door. Why did he have to be such a womanising jerk? And if he *had* changed then why in hell was he settling for Vivian? Rather than...

Meg closed the door behind her, loath even to look at the woman in her office. But her eyes were masochistically drawn. Vivian sat elegantly on the sofa with her long legs crossed, her arms folded over her breasts and her eyes narrowed.

'You called him Jake,' she asserted. Her perfect lips were pouting, her fine eyebrows arched and her chin tossed high. 'He doesn't let anyone call him Jake.'

'Oh?' Meg walked over to her desk and flicked open her pad. She wished she hadn't dashed out the door like that. If she hadn't asked Jake, he couldn't have blamed her if she'd blabbed everything to Vivian. 'What sort of dress did you want?'

'I told you—an evening gown for the charity gala.' Vivian slunk across the room. 'But I guess you were pretty busy eyeing up *my* Jacob. You know Jacob, don't you?'

'How did you guess?'

'You called him Jake,' she said impatiently. 'And that secretary said *again*.'

'Yes, I know him.' There was nothing else she could say—the woman *had* asked. But why hadn't Jake told Vivian about her? Her mind screamed in confusion. Nothing made sense. Least of all her feelings for her soon-to-be-ex-husband.

'No, he didn't tell me. Really, you think he might have earlier. I love your work,' she said lightly, one eyebrow finely arched, her eyes still hooded. 'He just called and insisted he get me one of your designs. He's like that, you know. So generous.'

'He must love you very much.' Meg scored the paper with the pencil and bit her lip to stifle the groan in her throat.

'Of course.' Vivian relaxed and smiled a perfect toothpaste-ad smile.

Who wouldn't love her? She was perfect. Probably as rich as sin too, by the way she moved and spoke. It had been the best schools for this woman, no doubt about it. And she was out to land the best prize of a husband she could get her perfectly manicured nails into.

Meg drew the curves of the woman onto the page. 'Do you want sleeves or straps?'

'It's a summer affair; I don't want sleeves.'

'Have you set a wedding date?' Meg asked.

Vivian smiled. 'Jake hasn't said anything to me yet. I think he's got some loose ends to tie up. But I'm sure it won't be long.'

'Me too.' Meg's heart sank deeper. The loose ends were staring Vivian in the face. 'What colours do you prefer?'

'I love red, gold and green.' Vivian tipped her head at an angle. 'So where do you know him from?'

'I lived next door to him.' Meg sketched the shape of the dress over the figure on the page, concentrating on the task at hand. 'I have a lovely emerald-green fabric that would suit you beautifully.'

'How quaint. Your boy next door.' Vivian's eyes narrowed, and for the first time Meg got the distinct impression that she'd been pegged as competition. 'What was he like then?'

'Younger.' Meg slapped the sketch onto the coffee table.

Joyce knocked and entered the room. 'Tea?'

'Yes, thank you, Joyce.' Meg wished she could escape out of the door with her secretary and hide in the kitchenette with the coffee.

'Black,' Vivian snapped off-handedly. She cast a long, hard look at Meg.

Like her. Dark. What if this woman was just after his money, or his body, or both? What if she didn't love Jake at all? Meg shook her head. Why did *she* care?

Joyce closed the door quietly and Meg glanced at Vivian again. It wasn't her business who Jake chose to marry. If he wanted this woman then so be it. But if this was the sort of woman he was attracted to now, there wasn't much he'd kept of his past.

Danny's laughing face came to mind. He was dark-haired, like Jake, and if you didn't look too closely you'd think they were brothers. Only Jake had stronger, finer features, a more handsome face. They'd been inseparable—until her father would arrive home, and then Jake would be straight over the fence and under his feet while Danny would wander home alone. Later, when they were older, they'd get together and go to the pub, to parties and the football together.

Meg had no idea when the booze had taken over Jake's life. All she'd known was that he'd grab a beer when he got home and he'd go to the pub with Danny. But she'd been young, and it hadn't been until his mother, Moira, had voiced her concerns that she'd started to worry.

'This is a rough draft—what do you think?' Meg presented Vivian with the sketch and sat down gingerly beside the woman on the sofa.

'It's great, though I'd want it lower at the neck.' She looked at her own cleavage, smiling. 'I like to show off my assets.'

'Yes, we wouldn't want to miss them.' Meg swung her pencil across the page, lowering the neckline. 'So, the cut, the length, the straps...' She pointed to them with her pencil and Vivian leant closer, wafts of an exotic scent invading Meg's nostrils.

'Beautiful, but I want it to look more special.'

Meg smiled. Typical. She should be thankful the woman didn't want her to design her wedding dress.

Meg sketched a thin jacket onto the dress so that by the time she was finished it looked like a long-sleeved, high-necked gown.

'But I wanted...'

'Yes, I know.' Meg had wanted a lot of things too, but dreams like Jake didn't really come true; they were just illusions. Like the dress. 'You pull here.' She touched the pencil to the neckline 'And the whole top I've just drawn falls away, leaving you with what we started with.'

'Incredible. That's great.'

'So how did you meet him?' Meg asked out of courtesy. No, she was kidding herself. It was indisputable curiosity that urged the question from her mouth. She wanted to know what Jake was like now, if he was just the same, if doubts tortured Vivian as they had her.

'At the club,' Vivian said off-handedly, examining her perfectly manicured and painted nails as if the design of the dress might have chipped one.

'Club?'

'Yes, the golf club. Jacob loves his golf.'

Meg bit into the end of her pencil, sinking her teeth deep. Jake had said once that he'd like to play one day. So 'one day' had come. 'But he can't get much of a chance, what with his overseas commitments.'

'Overseas?' Vivian sat taller, her smile broadening. 'It has been a while since you last

met, hasn't it? No, Jacob's work commitments
are all local. Well, local to Brisbane.'

Meg tried to keep from biting the pencil
clean through. Jake grounded in one place?
Her scorn leeched out of her. Maybe Vivian
was the right woman for him—her throat
closed over at the irony that he'd never stayed
home for her.

The tea arrived, but Meg didn't want to sit
and chat with the woman. Her head was about
to split in two with the tension.

'Grab your tea and go with Joyce,' Meg
suggested. 'Joyce, could you take Ms Shelton
and get all her measurements, then take her to
look through our gown fabric samples? We're
thinking emerald-green...' Meg crossed her
fingers behind her back and sent Joyce a pleading look. She didn't normally delegate, or
palm clients off, but she was desperate to escape and this woman was definitely an ex-
ception.

Joyce raised one of her eyebrows. 'No problem, Megan.'

Vivian rose and smoothed out her skin-tight suit, making sure that both Meg and Joyce were watching her as she caressed her perfectly slender waist and hips. 'Oh, just in case I don't see you again...'

Meg had to concede that Vivian was canny. There was no way on earth she'd see Vivian again today if she successfully foisted her off onto Joyce, and *she* knew it.

'I want to invite you to a party.'

'Me?'

'Yes, Megan,' Vivian purred. 'I can call you Megan, can't I?'

'Yes, sure,' Meg managed through tight lips. Why not? Vivian was already on intimate terms with her husband. 'You can call me whatever you want.' As long as she could do the same.

Meg wasn't sure when she dozed off, but some time after throwing her hands over her face and collapsing onto the sofa in her office, she must have nodded off. Her restless nights had taken their toll.

She opened her eyes gingerly, the hairs on the back of her neck alert, her pulse rushing. She wasn't alone. She wanted to shrink down inside herself and hide from the awful premonition that she was about to come eye to eye with Vivian Shelton's perfect features, looking down on her scornfully for being a mere mortal after all.

Vivid green eyes looked at her with an intensity that sent her body on full alert. 'What?' Meg jumped up from the sofa, her blood heating. 'What are you doing here?'

'I came to ask whether you're going to come to the party.' Jake's voice was a velvet murmur, and his eyes danced with warmth and concern as he rose from where he knelt.

How long had he been there, watching her? She crossed her arms over her chest, her heart pounding fiercely. It made her uneasy that she'd been so vulnerable, so sleepy, so stupid!

'Vivian already…already asked me.' Meg straightened out her clothes and smoothed down her hair, which she expected looked like a rat's nest by the way she could pick wafts of it up out of the corners of her vision. 'Though why she would ask me anywhere, I have no idea.'

'I asked her to.'

Meg stared at him, her mind going numb, searching for a plausible explanation for this invitation. A warning voice whispered that it would end in nothing but more pain. *Cut your losses and abandon ship.*

'You didn't give her an answer.'

'I know.' She forced her legs into motion and moved away from Jake, straightening herself out and trying to coerce her mind into logical thought patterns.

'You're not giving me a straight answer either.'

'Sorry, but it's not possible for someone in my situation to just make a slap-dash decision. There are more people involved.'

It was as though she'd slapped him. 'Like a babysitter.' His eyes clouded.

'Yes. Like my babysitter!' For his son! It was as if she was suggesting murder judging by his reaction. 'They don't just grow on trees, and she has a life too.'

He took a deep breath and his eyes softened. 'Can you give me an indication whether you're going to come?'

Meg sighed. 'When is it?'

'Tomorrow night.'

'That's short notice,' she hedged. 'I'm a very busy woman, and Tommy—'

'Yes, I know. You've got lots of aspects to consider.' His gaze swept over her, his eyes full of yesterday's promises, and her body responded as if she were that young woman again too. Naive and innocent. Willing and wanton.

A delicious shudder heated her body. 'Why do you want me to come?' To taunt her with his perfect girlfriend and rub her nose in the fact he'd found someone, despite his severe shortcomings, while she remained alone?

He clasped both her hands in his. 'It would mean a lot to me.'

His warmth caressed her, radiating up her arms and into her chest. She couldn't talk, couldn't utter a word. Her breath left her body, her pulse-rate hiked, her palms tingled—and she couldn't tear her eyes away from his deep green eyes. 'Okay,' she whispered. 'I'll work it out.'

He thrust a hand in his pocket and pulled out a business card, placing it in her still tingling hands. 'This is the place. At eight.'

'Who do you know in Melbourne?'

'I know a few people here.' He eyed her, a smile tugging at his mouth. 'I'm not socially challenged, you know.'

The light in his eyes altered his whole persona. Meg's heart jolted and her pulse thundered through her veins. Charm and magnetism exuded from him like a drug.

'Why?' she asked again. She edged to the door. It was time to escape Jake's intoxicating presence before she did or said something she'd regret later. 'Why do you want me to come?'

'Why not?' He followed her.

'Jake.' She reached the door and stepped to one side, leaning against the wall to support her knees, which were rapidly turning to jelly. She forced herself to focus on Tommy. 'We need to have a talk some time, about Tommy.'

His features froze over and he shook his head. 'No. I've heard all I need to.' He yanked open the door. 'I don't want to hear another word about him.'

CHAPTER SIX

MEG slipped on her black dress and berated herself for agreeing to go to the party. She wasn't going to know anyone. If she was lucky, she could stand in some corner and pretend to be a potted plant. If she was unlucky, she could talk to the only people she would know—Vivian and Jake. Either way she was in for an arduous evening.

Meg wriggled her toes into another pair of stockings and slowly shimmied them up her legs. It was her last pair, and if they didn't make it without mishap this time she would take it as a sign that she wasn't meant to go, or that she should wear trousers.

The problem was that her hands refused to behave. They had started to tremble at about five o'clock and had continued to wreak havoc on her façade of calm and control through three pairs of stockings.

Meg eyed her legs carefully for runs. She let out her breath. Made it. But she wasn't sure whether to be happy about it or not.

She yanked open the box for her new black shoes. With fine straps interlacing, and a heel to make her tall enough to look into any man's face, she hadn't been able to resist them when she'd been in the shoe shop last month. She would never have guessed she'd be wearing them out with Jake and his girlfriend.

Meg stepped into the shoes and perused herself in the mirror. She'd blow-dried her short blonde hair into a wild but trendy mess and her dress hugged her generous frame, emphasising every curve, running full length to her ankles with sexy slits up the sides to make the most of her legs. Not bad, but she'd never match Vivian.

Some part of her wished the woman had some obvious flaws, so she could have felt as if she had some claim, but no, life didn't work that way.

Tommy's room was dimly lit. Meg could see his assorted stuffed animals lined up on his shelf, the jungle prints she'd painted on the wall and the deep blue blanket crumpled at the end of his cot. She tucked the blanket up over his chest. He had the habit of kicking his covers off, even if it was freezing.

She smiled at his innocent form. His thumb lay close to his mouth, still wet from its last impersonation of a dummy. She touched his cheek lightly and felt her throat close over and the tears sting her eyes. Why didn't Jake care?

Meg heard the babysitter move around downstairs.

She kissed the end of her finger and touched her little boy's forehead, then crept out of the room before her emotional state sent ripples careering into Tommy's sensors. If he woke now she'd never get out the door. She glanced at her watch; she was already running late.

Meg hesitated. She *could* pull Tommy's leg—that way she wouldn't have to go… But a large chunk of her insisted she should go through with this masochism, for old times' sake.

Seeing Jake with Vivian, socialising and all over each other, would bring her back to reality, drive it into her heart that Jake had gone on without her. It would signify the end of their relationship, such as it was, and make her realise that it was now time for her to have a real life of her own.

A dull emptiness echoed inside her. Who could she find to fill Jake's place? For all his faults, she had the suspicion that no one ever would.

The music throbbed through the street. Meg climbed from the taxi, willing her feet to keep moving even when the obvious luxury of the neighbourhood intimidated her. Although she was meant to be up and coming in the world of fashion, she felt more at home with sewing machines than parties.

Elegant Mercedes, Saabs, Volvos, BMWs and the occasional Porsche lined the road in front of the driveway of the mansion. Lamps along the drive highlighted the impeccably kept lawns and gardens.

Meg watched a couple saunter up the walk, the woman in a full-length fur coat, the greying gentleman beside her in a dark suit.

Meg swallowed hard. She was out of her league here. For a second she had the urge to leap over the rock border and tramp right through the flowerbed, to show that she was an individual, not to be herded and typecast. But her feet betrayed her by following several paces behind the couple, stuck in her conservatism, and she hated herself for it.

Anxiety gnawed at her. Why had Jake wanted her to come?

The place looked as if it was rendered brick, painted white with large columns boldly announcing the front door. It was three storeys high, judging by the myriad of lights in the windows above her, and long—too long to possibly use all the rooms unless they were bed and breakfasting or running a museum.

There was a butler at the door.

Meg's confidence dropped to her toes. She stepped back into the shadows while the couple just ahead of her disappeared inside. She could count the seconds with her heartbeat, pounding against her bones.

The music poured out of the door in a torrent, mingled with the chatter of a large group of people who sounded like a hundred pigeons all in one cage.

Meg shifted on her feet, the backs of her shoes already scoring their mark into her flesh. She couldn't see the ceiling of the foyer, but an extra large chandelier hung about two and a half metres from the fountain in pride of place in the middle. A carpet-covered staircase curved upward at the rear of the impossibly large entry, scattered with people.

Paintings and tapestries hung on the walls Meg could see from her vantage point, the pastel cream paint highlighting the brilliance of colour used by the artisans. The whole place reeked 'filthy rich and flaunting it'.

The staid butler coughed. 'Good evening, madam.'

Meg stepped out of the shadows and onto the white marble floor, her head held high. 'I've had better.'

The butler leant closer to her. 'I know what you mean.'

She smiled and let him take her velvet coat from her. It was nothing more than a wrap with sleeves for the balmy summer evening. The woman who'd come in before her must have gratefully disposed of her fur coat, glad not to have melted into a puddle before she reached the door.

'Meg.' Jake's voice caressed her name with warmth.

Her spine tingled in response. She turned and couldn't help but gape at him. His muscular body was perfectly adorned in a black evening suit that jolted Meg back to their wedding day with such force and clarity it was hard for her not to reach out for him.

She averted her eyes and scanned the crowd. He'd moved up a few more notches than she'd imagined. Her gaze wandered back to her husband, to how his dark hair was combed back severely, showing off his high forehead and emphasising his sexy eyes. She swallowed the lump of desire and managed a smile.

'Glad to see me?' His eyebrows were drawn together and he sounded hesitant.

'Sure I am. I feel like a fish out of water and you're the only person I know here.' Meg was glad she had a good excuse. The truth was she wanted to run into his arms for some perverse reason. Telling herself it was for him to protect her from all these strange people seemed easier than confronting the feelings she was trying so hard to suppress.

'You surprise me, Meg. I thought you'd be at this sort of do every week.'

'No.' Meg held her hands together tightly. 'I have other commitments.' Which always sounded so damn good on the phone, when she was getting out of one of these dos, but didn't later when she counted how many sales she might have lost. Her life was such a balancing act, and she felt she was dropping too much.

'Yes, of course. How stupid of me.'

Damn, she hated reminding him all the time of Tommy, but she had to. It was eating away at her, him ignoring his son this way. She chewed her bottom lip, casting a glance at Jake's grim face.

She turned around to face the crowd. It was hard to take in the many suited men, all milling about in their blacks, greys and blues, some tall, some short, some handsome and the rest trying to pretend they were.

The women were fascinating. Meg instantly recognised the designs of Christian Dior, Versace, Karan and Prada, and she even saw one of her own that made her stand just that little bit taller. Nearly everyone wore gowns, save a couple of women impeccably dressed in business suits.

Meg loved the colours. The range of reds especially fascinated her. They dotted the scene from crimson to blood-red. She snapped her eyes back as she caught a glimpse of Vivian in the most vibrant blood-red gown. 'Do you know these people?'

'I know some of them,' Jake responded matter-of-factly.

'Are you going to let me in on why you invited me?' Her throat tightened and she hoped her voice sounded half-normal.

'Not yet.' He sort of smiled, radiating an air of calm and confidence, then Jake stepped forward and took her hand.

His touch sent a buzzing electric current zinging up her arm into her spine, dancing through her nervous system like a rogue bee.

Meg resisted the urge to yank her hand from him—it meant nothing. Her body was merely suffering a lack of male attention. 'Are you rich, Jake?'

'Rich?' He laughed—genuinely laughed. His whole face transformed, the hard lines becoming softer, his eyes glittering, his mouth warm and soft and inviting.

She couldn't help but smile. 'Is that a joke?'

'Yes.' Jake turned away from her and pulled her through the crowd, weaving expertly past strangers' faces that blurred into one big mass.

'You didn't answer me,' Meg blurted as they swept around a huddle of six trendy young up-and-comings, with champagne flutes in hand and mobile phones on hip.

'I have my own business.'

So Vivian had been on the level about Jake giving up his overseas adventures for Aussie-based ones. 'But this?' she chivvied. 'Surely this is out of your league?'

His feet stopped and he swung around and glared at her. 'Of course. I'm only some cowboy construction guy with no brains.' The hurt burned in his eyes and his fingers tightened their grip on her hand.

She swallowed the sob that rose in her throat. 'You were.' He'd never shown her anything else.

Jake dropped her hand as if it was a burning coal, as if he couldn't get rid of her fast enough. 'I was a lot more than that.' His voice broke. 'I expected more of you, Meg.'

She bit her lip. It had come out all wrong. She hadn't meant to hurt him, and if she had she hadn't meant for him to turn on her and throw her own flaws back at her. She looked at his polished black shoes.

'Come and say hello to a few people.' His voice was cold and proud. They were next to a crowd of twelve, mostly in their forties, some greying, all superbly dressed, the women covered in jewels.

Icy fingers seeped into Meg's every pore and she steadfastly refused to look at Jake. This was it. Fed to the wolves.

As soon as Jake introduced Meg she was more popular than chocolate—which shocked her fear right out of her. She was passed from one group to the next like a platter of goodies, to be sampled by everyone wanting to try the latest flavour.

It was great for a little while, then her feet started to ache, reminding her of their plight in taming the audacious shoes. Even her love of talking about fabrics and designs couldn't dull the discomfort, and it all became repetitious and monotonous. And then there was Jake's face, hovering in the crowd, continually putting her off what she was saying, reminding her of the precarious position she was in.

The nagging question of why he'd invited her kept playing on her mind. Was he trying to prove how far he'd come, fitting into this suave, sophisticated environment? Or was he flaunting how much he'd changed for Vivian in her face?

Meg slipped through a gap while someone else was introduced, and was just looking for some corner to escape to when someone grabbed her arm.

'Come with me,' Jake whispered, his breath hot against her ear.

Her whole body lurched. Waves of awareness rippled through her, and she let herself be steered across the room when all the while her mind shouted warnings.

Meg saw Vivian standing by a large exotic plant. She was tall and stunning in the red satin dress that hugged her figure. Meg had considered wearing a red gown of her own, but it was far too flamboyant for the possibilities of this situation. It wasn't as if she was inviting passion and heat. Not like Vivian.

She hung back a little, dragging on Jake's arm. He was going too fast for her to concoct some witty repartee.

Jake turned. 'What is it?' He was impatient.

A wave of nausea washed over her. 'I think it's time for me to go home.' She just couldn't bring herself to see Jake and Vivian together, intimately wrapped in each other.

'The best is just about to start.' He tugged her arm again.

Meg cast him an enquiring look, trying to read the importance of his aloofness. What was she in store for? Another wave attacked.

'Vivian,' Meg acknowledged as they stopped at the group where Vivian was animatedly talking.

'Megan, darling. I'm so glad you're here.' She looked fondly over Meg's shoulder at Jake and smiled. 'We've got a surprise for you.'

Meg felt ill. They were up to something and she was stuck in the middle, with Jake covering her back in case of escape. She must have caused him so much anguish by vanishing like she did. Visions of him exacting revenge, nasty and sickeningly sweet, came to mind.

Vivian stepped back, out of Meg's line of vision. Nothing registered except the ache in her heart and her feet. The hazy image of a dark-haired guy coming towards her triggered her to focus. She was obviously his target.

The features became sharper, his face distinct and familiar. Hazel eyes, cheeky grin and a dark lock of hair hanging down onto his forehead. 'Oh, my God!' Meg's feet flew forward. 'Danny!'

Danny opened his arms wide and she dived into his embrace. It had been for ever since she'd seen him. She wrapped her arms around him, noticing there was a fair bit more of him than when she'd last hugged him.

She could hear his heart with her ear. He felt so warm and so good she didn't want to let him go—he'd protect her from this lot— the 'lot' who were watching now. Meg stepped back self-consciously.

Danny held her by the shoulders. 'Let me get a good look at you.'

Meg smiled coyly. It was like being on parade for your relatives, when they tell you you've grown up so much—though Jake wasn't looking anywhere as thrilled about the reunion as Meg had expected him to. It was such a great surprise!

'Well, I can't say you've grown, but you've matured all right. No more puppy fat.'

'Gee, thanks,' she sniped, throwing her hands on her hips. She couldn't help but keep smiling, although she felt as if her face might crack from the strain of it.

Danny touched her shortly cropped hair. 'You cut it.'

She'd had long hair all her life, *and* when she'd married Jake. It had been a beautiful white wedding, with a church full of friends. Meg faltered. And it had all been a lie.

Jake clenched his fists, digging what nails he had into his palms. Meg was certainly glad to see Danny. All she'd given *him* was harsh words, and she'd hated the sight of him so much she'd hidden behind a bloody menu.

His hurt turned into white-hot anger. There *was* something between them. It was all Jake could do to stop himself reaching for Dan's neck.

He watched Dan's arms wrap around her. How could she let him touch her like that? God, he wanted a hug like that. He would have died and gone to heaven to have her throw herself into his arms.

At least he'd stolen that kiss. *Stolen it*. Jake stifled the urge to yell. *Meg loved Dan*. She had to. He was the father of her baby, after all. The thought left him with an inexplicable feeling of emptiness.

'Jake called up to say you guys were in town.' Dan spoke eagerly and Meg was hanging on every word.

Meg shifted her weight and Jake's body reacted. She looked so sexy in that black dress it was all he could do to stay in control. Each time she moved his eyes would dart to her shape, moving under the thin fabric, and his blood would heat and every curve would beckon to him. He longed to run his hands down her body like he used to.

The soft roundness of the tops of her breasts peeked out from the gown, taunting him with their fullness and perfection. He found himself remembering how well their bodies had fitted together once, and tried very hard to stop imagining her on their wedding night in that silken white negligee. He could feel his temperature rising at the mere thought.

'And is there a little woman and kids at home waiting for you?' Meg asked Dan, her voice cheerful.

Jake's blood ceased flowing. He'd figured it would be one of the first questions she'd ask if she was besotted with the jerk. He had to hand it to her—she had done well, disguising her interest with mild curiosity, sizing up the competition before she put herself on the line. Jake already knew the answer. He'd grilled Dan before inviting him to the party and back into Meg's life.

It was the last thing in the world he wanted to do. Hand Meg to another man—the same one who had ruined his life and hers—but he had to make it right for her.

'No, divorced.' Dan slid his hand slowly down her bare shoulder and down her arm to clasp her hand. 'No kids.'

'I'm sorry.' Meg squeezed his fingers.

'Better not to have them when things get messed up.'

Jake saw that Dan didn't look at him. Or couldn't. Dan had to know how his betrayal hurt him. For years he'd trusted Dan to look out for Meg, like a brother, but she wasn't his sister and Dan wasn't a saint. Jake should have seen it coming.

Jake's guts tossed. The arguments he'd had with Meg about him staying home longer... And he'd refused. He'd been hell-bent on learning all the tricks of the job, on being the best, assuming she'd always be there for him. He was an idiot. He hadn't seen the warnings. It was obvious now how unhappy she'd been. Obvious with Meg's little son at home, waiting for her.

Meg darted a look at Jake and his nerves jangled. 'Yes,' she said quietly, her eyes hooded. 'Better not to have children when there are problems.'

Why was she looking at him? It wasn't as if he'd fathered the kid. It might have been his fault, but he hadn't got her into *that* situation. Jake glared at Dan, balling his fists at his sides. It should've been him, Jake, who was the father of her child.

If only Dan had kept his filthy hands off her.

Vivian's arm slid around Jake's waist and she brushed herself against him. 'They make such a sweet couple,' she whispered, leaning close.

Jake saw Meg's eyes dart to him. What was she thinking? He'd love to be able to read her mind. He could read her body. And her body liked him. But obviously it liked Dan more. There was none of that stand-offishness with Dan. She'd leapt straight into his arms. He felt like throwing up his heart to rid him of the pain.

All those years of fantasising about finding her, her being proud of the man he'd become, having her fall into his arms and kiss him soundly, telling him she was sorry and swearing undying love to him. He gulped at his own stupidity.

Dan swung his arm across Meg's back and his hand rested on her bare skin, cupping her naked shoulder. Jake clenched his fists, trying to quell the thoughts of Dan's hands running over her body, of the baby they'd made together, and it was all he could do to stay rooted to the spot.

'You set this up,' Meg accused Jake, wrapping her arm around Dan's waist as if Jake wasn't even there.

Had she no shame? Did it mean nothing to her that he was still her husband, if in name only?

'Yes,' Vivian tittered, ignoring Jake's silence. 'We wanted to surprise you. We knew you and Dan were close and you'd *love* to see him.'

Jake couldn't miss the wink Vivian sent him. She'd come back from Meg's office asking for explanations of their relationship so she'd know how to play her role. He'd decided to come clean—to a degree. To tell her that Meg was a close friend who'd a crush on his best mate and was a victim of unrequited love.

Vivian had been of terrific help. She'd been eager to help him find Dan and get him to Melbourne as soon as possible. Jake figured she considered it romantic to be a part of making it right again and seemed to thrive on the challenge. If only he could feel the same.

'I'm thrilled.' Meg smiled into Danny's face.

The smile knifed Jake from his loins to his heart. His breath burned in his throat. Why wasn't that smile for him?

'You'll want to catch up.' Vivian hooked her arm through Jake's. 'You must have so much news. We'll leave you two alone.' She tossed a look around the crowded room. 'Well, as alone as you'll get just at the moment.' She laced her words with such a heavy dose of innuendo she might as well have stripped them naked and shoved them towards a bed.

Vivian led Jake away and he followed helplessly, his feet leaden. All he wanted to do was punch the guy in the face, throw Meg over his shoulder and go home. He suppressed his instincts and let himself be dragged into the throng.

He glanced behind but they were already lost in the bustle of people. He wanted to go back. Do something. He itched to do something. But he'd destroyed her life last time round—the least he could do was give Meg and Dan this time together. Leave them alone.

He watched her.

His eyes were drawn to her.

He'd slowly inched across the room whilst talking to some of Vivian's friends so he could see her. It was torture to watch her lean over on the sofa they'd secured for themselves. She was so close to him, whispering sweet nothings in Dan's ear while he smiled like the bloody Cheshire cat from hell.

Jake shook his watch. Time seemed to have stood still. The hands weren't moving no matter how many times he checked it.

Vivian grabbed his wrist and glared at him. 'You'd think he was stealing the royal jewels. Relax.' She pulled him out onto the back patio with the dancing couples.

He forced his feet to move, but he was a lousy dancer at the best of times, and he was so distracted by the idea of what they were getting up to away from his watchful eyes that it made counting impossible.

'Jake!' Vivian's yelp echoed in his ear. 'They'll be fine. They're not exactly kids and you're not their father.'

But I'm her husband, he wanted to say. But he wouldn't shock Vivian by blurting it out right now. She'd done a lot to help him and she deserved the whole story—later.

Jake caught a glimpse of Meg, alone, weaving through the crowd. His feet froze, one on top of Vivian's. 'Pitstop,' he offered, and backed away from her.

He was so confused. Logic said to leave Meg to Dan, to let her tell him about the baby, make it right, but his body burned with desire—he wanted her more than anything he'd ever wanted. If there was a chance she didn't love Dan…

'Fine.' Vivian was obviously just tolerating him and his erratic behaviour. 'I'll be here, waiting.'

Jake found Meg coming out of the bathroom, smoothing down her black dress, her hands running the wrinkles down her hips and thighs, emphasising their perfection.

She almost walked into him. 'Sorry,' she offered, and went to move around him.

It was as though she didn't even want to know him. He didn't blame her. He'd been a jerk. 'Meg.' His voice came out too deep.

She looked up, eyes wide. She hadn't known it was him! His breath rushed from his lungs.

'Jake.' His name was a sigh on her lips.

He drank in her nearness, her perfume, the scent of roses drifting to him, calling to him, pulling him into her magnetic gravity. He saw the heart-rending tenderness in her gaze, as soft as a caress, and his blood hammered through his veins.

He cleared his throat, pretending not to be affected.

She ran her tongue along her full lips. 'Jake, I...' Her eyes caught his.

A shiver of wanting ran through him.

His mouth swooped down and captured hers, and he pulled her into his arms, crushing her to his body.

CHAPTER SEVEN

MEG was shocked at her own eager response to his kiss. He was plying her lips with such a demanding mastery that she couldn't help but part her own, opening herself to his exploration.

The kiss sang through her body, awakening her to the memories of Jake's touch, and desire ached in the pit of her stomach, in her loins and in every beat of her heart. Meg couldn't help herself. She kissed him back, savouring every moment.

Jake tasted hot and sweet, with a slight hint of champagne. She melted into his arms, abandoning her mind in favour of the sensations running wild within her.

She ran her hands up his back and the ripple of his muscles played beneath her fingers. There was a dreamy intimacy to the kiss and her knees became weak. It was as if it was their first kiss, as if the past didn't exist at all.

Her mind jerked to sanity. She pushed her hands against his chest, shoving his body away. 'No!'

'What?' Jake pulled back, lust burning in his eyes.

Her stomach tightened. 'What do you mean *what*? How dare you kiss me like that? And don't tell me my lips were begging for it, because they weren't.'

'You liked it.'

She stared at his black tie as her cheeks heated. 'So you can kiss. Congratulations. What do you think that makes you—God's gift to women?'

'Of course not, Meg.' The rich timbre of his voice echoed down her veins and her lips tingled. 'I just…'

'Yeah, right.' Meg wrenched herself out of his arms. 'And your girlfriend's right there.' She threw an accusing finger down the hall. 'Sounds like a familiar scenario?' She paused, searing him with her eyes. 'After all, you can't help yourself but kiss *all* the girls.'

'What are you talking about, Meg?'

She had his attention now, but she had no idea what to do with it. She lifted her chin and spun on her heels and strode to where she'd left Danny. He was lounging back in the seat, his eyes half closed.

'Can we get out of here?'

'Sure, where do you want to go?'

'Home. Let's go to my place.' Meg figured she'd get some peace there. She spun around towards the door and found Jake, blocking her path. Her heart skipped a beat and she had the urge to touch her still tingling lips. 'Come on, Danny.' She looked straight into Jake's face, hoping her icy façade stayed intact. 'Let's go.'

Meg sauntered through the crowd, swinging her hips in wild abandon, totally aware of Jake's eyes glued to her. So he wanted her. Tough! She was never going to let him touch her again.

Vivian ran a hand over Jake's arm, moving her body close beside his. 'That went well.'

Jake nodded, staring at the door, a wild raw grief filling him. It was like losing her all over again and he was just as helpless.

Anger burned in him. *Meg thought he'd had affairs.*

He let his shoulders drop. It didn't matter... Meg was with Dan now. There wasn't any room for him. No chance for him to have a life, any sort of life, with Meg. And that was all that really mattered...

'I've always liked you, Meg.' Danny moved closer to her, into the gentle light on her doorstep.

'I know.' Meg rustled in her bag for her key. She could hear her heart still pounding in her chest from Jake's kiss. Her breath was uneven, her head was starting to ache and her heart was creaking, ready to break all over again if she let it.

'No, Meg. You don't.' There was an edge to his voice. 'I mean I *really* liked you.' His voice throaty and hesitant.

'You did?' Meg was surprised. For all of Danny's visits, their quiet talks, she'd never guessed. She'd figured Jake had requested him to check up on her, not that he had interests of his own. She plucked her keys out and fumbled for the lock, stepping close to the door.

'And I still do.' His breath fanned her neck.

Meg turned. 'That's so sweet Danny.' Meg was all for telling him that she was ruined for life. That the one and only man she'd ever loved was gone, he was a womanising ratbag and he'd never loved her in the first place, but Danny knew that already. 'But I'm kind of really bogged down in things at the moment. I'm trying to get my label off the ground.'

'I've heard you're doing a pretty bang-up job.'

She shrugged. She supposed she had been doing okay until Mrs Bolton's nephew had decided she had to pull her funds. Now her business was a mess. She had to admit she'd probably got too cocky because of Mrs Bolton's generosity, and now she was weighed down with a whole heap of debt and not a whole lot of cashflow.

'Is there a chance you might be interested in me some time in the future?'

Meg gave him a long look. He was nice-looking, and kind, and he made a great friend, but she couldn't see herself wrapped in his arms until death did they part—not with Jake around, not ever. She shook her head.

Danny leant towards her, capturing her lips.

Meg pulled back, pressing her hands onto his chest. 'No, Danny. What are you doing?'

'I had to kiss you, Meg. I've thought about it for so long.'

She'd never realised. The significance of his words struck her. It wasn't just a fancy—it was real! Heat flooded her cheeks and her mind grappled to take it in. Had everything he'd told her been coloured by his attraction to her? 'I'm sorry. You're a great guy but—' How could she explain her affections for him were like that of a sister?

'You're stuck on someone else.' Danny leant over and kissed her lightly on the cheek, putting his arms around her. 'I didn't think I had a chance. You're still wrapped up in Jake, aren't you.'

'Is it that obvious?' she whispered.

'Obvious to me—yes. I know you both so well. Look, I need to tell you…' He hesitated, then stepped back. Finally, he pressed a slip of paper into her palm.

She closed her fingers over the note and he stepped off the porch and into the darkness.

'If you need a friend.'

Meg watched the red tail-lights of his car fade up the street before she turned and pushed her key into the lock.

Part of her had wanted to take up Danny's offer. He had always been safer and more predictable than Jake—and she would have loved to rub an affair in Jake's face for once, to see if he liked how it felt. But that made the erroneous assumption that he cared in the first place.

A hand clasped down on her shoulder. 'What the hell are you playing at?'

She knew Jake's voice as well as she knew her own. He was livid. 'What?' She turned and propped her hands on her hips. She was so sick of this game of his. She had no idea what rules he was playing by, but she knew she wasn't faring well.

'Dan was here, on your doorstep, ready, willing and able. And you sent him away?' There was a bitter edge of cynicism in his voice.

Had Jake expected her to take Danny to her bed? Jake must think she was a desperate frustrated woman. Her cheeks flooded with heat. Had he called Danny to let him know she was an easy score?

An uneasy queasiness rolled into her belly as she swung around to face him. She stood taller and tried to look him in the eye. 'I'd like to point out that I'm quite capable of finding a man of my own, if I wanted one. Thanks anyway.'

'Hell, no, Meg.' He raked a hand over his chin and through his hair. 'I just thought you and Dan... You didn't even invite him in to see the kid.'

'The kid?' she echoed. He was referring to his own child as *the kid*. She closed her eyes and suddenly the weight on her shoulders seemed too much to bear. She'd been right. He didn't deserve a child—least of all a son. Her own father popped into her mind, the bitter irony of him desperately wanting a son and his wife. Jake had both and wanted neither.

'Why didn't you show him? Did you tell him?' His tone was rough and coolly disapproving, his eyes sharp and assessing, fixed on her.

Meg became increasingly uncomfortable under his scrutiny. 'No. Why should I?' Her mind raced to try and unscramble the significance of his line of questioning, but her brain failed her.

'What about responsibility?'

Meg eyed him. Finally! 'What about it?' It wasn't as if she wanted him to pay Tommy's way, but some acknowledgment of his responsibility would be nice. She almost laughed.

She'd been so afraid when he first saw his son that he'd go overboard with his inflated sense of duty, and now she was almost praying for it.

He raked his hand through his hair. 'You don't love Dan, do you?'

'What sort of question is that?' She was startled. 'No, of course not. Whatever gave you that idea?'

Jake looked confused. 'You ran.'

'I didn't run because I was in love with Danny, Jake.'

'You didn't?' He almost choked on the words.

Meg stepped backwards, pressing her body against the timber door. It swung open and she staggered.

'Then *why* did you run?' It was almost a whisper.

Meg recovered her balance and gripped the cool metal of the door handle for support. She had no trouble answering that one. She wasn't a naive little girl any more, who couldn't say boo—she was a woman and she was sick of being diplomatic. Jake didn't care a hoot about Tommy! 'Because I couldn't stand to be married to someone who didn't love me,' she bit out. 'Who drank like a fish and slept with every girl he could get his bloody lips near.'

'What?' Jake stood stock still. The only part of him that moved were his eyes. He seared her with them. 'What the hell are you talking about, Meg?'

She felt her throat close over and her eyes stung mercilessly. 'You know exactly what I'm talking about. Everybody knew about it.'

His chest expanded and he straightened to his full height, his hands clenching into fists. 'Who?'

Meg stepped back at the severity of his tone. 'They all knew.' A sob escaped from her. 'I was the only dope that didn't see it. Of course Danny knew. You probably told him all about every one of them.'

'Dan?' he growled, his face darkening.

'And even your own mother knew what you were up to.' Meg almost gagged on the words. Hearing of her husband's sordid exploits from his mother was the worst nightmare she'd ever lived through. 'You should never have married me, Jake.' She was unable to hold in the agony any more. 'You never loved me.' And she slammed the door shut in his face.

Meg didn't and still doesn't love Dan, Jake thought wildly. His mind battled with confusion and disbelief at his own stupidity for accepting Meg's leaving him. He'd been so filled with rage at how efficiently he'd continued to screw up his life, and hers, just like his parents had, that he hadn't seen the game his own mother and Danny had played on his young wife. Until now.

He rapped on the hotel door with such force and severity it was a wonder he didn't crack a knuckle.

Meg had accused him of so much it made his head whirl. But first things first. Meg didn't love Danny. That could mean only one thing.

The door swung open. 'Jake.' Dan wore a smile on his face.

Jake clenched his fist. Dan had got Meg drunk, fed her stories of his supposed infidelities and taken advantage of her. He punched Dan in the face.

Dan grabbed at his nose. 'What the hell—?'

'That's for Meg,' he snarled. He turned and strode down the hallway, a lump caught in his throat.

Jake wrapped a towel around his hand, the ice clinking inside as he arranged it over his knuckles. He stabbed the numbers on the phone.

'What the hell's been going on, Mother? I've just seen Meg and she tells me I'm some two-timing bastard.' Dan's betrayal was one thing, his mother's another.

'Meg?' There was a long pause. 'You know how that girl tells stories all the time.'

'No, I don't know that. I've never heard her lie.' She was the sweetest, most loving person he knew. Sure, she was spirited, and sometimes stubborn as all hell, but he figured he knew her pretty well. At least he'd thought he did. Until she'd run away from him. Jake shook his head. He was driving himself mad.

'You think I lied to her?' Moira's voice rose in pitch.

'There's a good chance you lied to her, but I have no idea why.' His mother was renowned for her fickleness and her manipulative ways. Jake had seen her on numerous occasions twist situations to suit her designs, or blatantly lie to get into or out of something. He figured she wouldn't have hesitated for a moment to do the same with Meg—for a reason. What it was, he couldn't fathom…

'Son, I'm hurt,' she moaned. 'You don't even trust your own mother.'

'Come on. I know you pretty well. Why did you do it?' It wasn't as though she'd ignored his relationships before. When he'd paraded girlfriends past his mother she'd always found something to complain or comment about—their hair, or teeth, or clothes and manners. He was glad he hadn't given her a chance with Meg.

She cleared her throat. 'I did it for you, honey.'

He swallowed the rising anger in his gut. '*Why* did you do it?'

'I knew you didn't love her.'

'How the hell did you figure that one?' He still hadn't worked out whether what he felt was love. The tearing ache in his chest could be love, but after all that he'd been through as a child he had no idea what love really was. He'd always lusted for Meg, but he'd known she was something special and hadn't done anything about it until after her father had died.

'Sure she was good-looking, son. And I'm sure she was okay in bed...'

'Mum!'

'I heard Danny and you talking about her father.' Her voice hardened. 'How he died—how you promised. I couldn't have you waste your life like that.'

Jake's heart clenched tight. Meg's dad had told Jake he was like a son to him and that he was so proud of him—no one, not one of his mother's partners, had ever been around long enough to even care, let alone be proud. It had been the best moment of his life, and the worst.

George had coughed up blood, and his eyes had glazed over. He'd reached for Jake's shirt and tugged him close. *'Look after my Meg, Jake. Promise me you'll look after my Meg.'* His dying words had clung to him.

'That was none of your business.' He'd only shared it with Dan because he'd wanted to impress upon him the importance of looking after Meg. When he'd come back from that job he'd supported Meg through the funeral. She'd changed so much, filled out at every curve from the gangly schoolgirl he'd known. He'd been hooked. When he'd headed off to the next job he'd thought of nothing but her, and the next trip home he'd swept her off her feet. They'd married only a month later.

'I'm your mother. Your life is my business.'

'I appreciate your concern, but stay out of it.' His tone was relatively civil, despite his swamping anger. How could she possibly think she was qualified to interfere in his life when hers was a constant mess? And now his was too.

What chance did their marriage have now? A stab of guilt pierced his chest. How was he going to help Meg when she thought he was a womanising creep?

A chill black silence surrounded him. He shook his head. He needed time to work out his next move…

He gripped the phone tighter. 'You didn't tell Meg, did you?' A cold knot formed deep inside him. 'About the promise I made.'

'No.' His mother coughed. 'Just about the girls.'

'What bloody girls?'

CHAPTER EIGHT

MEG finally tossed herself into a fitful sleep, waking in the early hours to Tommy's crying. She threw back the sheet and struggled into a dressing gown, her mind and body protesting.

The dull light of approaching sunrise lit his room. He stood teary-eyed, hanging onto the side of the cot, his teddy bear on the floor. 'Mama get,' he called, reaching for his fuzzy friend.

Meg picked up the teddy and lifted her son into her arms. His hot *fragrant* nappy was weighing him down. She laid him on the change-mat on the floor. 'How are you this morning, sweetheart?'

Tommy cooed.

'Mummy had a strange night, honey. She saw your daddy, but he's still in denial.' Meg yanked off his offensive nappy, wrinkling her nose.

'Mama.' Tommy gave her a quizzical look while she discarded the wet nappy and wiped him down.

'Mummy thinks she still loves your daddy.' It had popped out, unbidden, from the recesses of her subconscious. The admission made out loud was strange, even to her own ears. She'd been trying to convince herself for years that her love for Jake was gone, and in some way it was a relief to say it and in another scary.

The doorbell rang.

She plucked a new nappy from the drawer, fastened it and pulled a fresh pair of track pants onto Tommy. 'Who's up this early?' She gathered her son into her arms.

Meg balanced Tommy on her hip and went downstairs. She plopped him onto the living room rug in his playpen.

She opened the door. Smiling hazel eyes danced at Meg from beneath a wild mane of auburn hair. Suzie wore a black singlet, grey shorts and sneakers. Her skin was covered in a sheen that suggested she'd been jogging and her cherry lips sported a smile as she waggled her finger at Meg.

'Suzie!' It was just like her. Nothing for days, then voilà, standing on the doorstop with a bakery bag of aromatic goodies and a grin a mile wide.

Suzie darted a look into the hall and up the stairs. 'So where is he?'

'Tommy?'

'No, your hunk from the restaurant—your Jake. He has to be here. He wasn't going to take no for an answer, you know.' Her eyes glinted with mischief. She was practically drooling and her eyes glowed with the possibilities her mind was feverishly feeding her.

'I know.' Meg raised her eyes skyward. 'And he's the most arrogant son of a—'

Suzie ignored her and waltzed into the hall and then into the lounge, making the sort of noise in the back of her throat that sounded like, 'Yeah, sure, and pigs fly'. She greeted Tommy with a series of distinct and noisy animal calls.

Tommy looked at Suzie with wide eyes for a moment. He cocked his head, then decided she was safe, smiled and went back to arranging his blocks of wood into a tower.

'So, are you finally going to tell me all the gossip? About your mysterious past?' Suzie dropped onto her sofa. 'Where do you know him from? He sort of acted as though he knew you really well—what's he like in bed?'

'Suzie!' Trust her to get straight to the juicy bits. Meg's mind darted back and relived their wedding night in detail. She could feel her blood heat and she shook her head. 'What's there to say? He's Tommy's father.'

'I knew it! Does he know? Did you leave him because you were pregnant and he didn't want the baby? Or didn't you know until you'd gone? Did you tell him then? What did he say?'

'Yes, he knows.' Meg's voice threatened to pack it in. 'I told him.'

'And...?'

'And nothing.' Tears sprang to her eyes and traitorously rolled down her cheeks. 'He doesn't want to know anything about him.' Or her, for that matter. He had his precious Vivian now and nothing else mattered. Not even a son.

Suzie crossed her arms. 'What a jerk!'

'He even had the nerve to set me up with his best mate so he wouldn't have to pay me so much money.' Meg choked on the words. He'd wanted her to sleep with Danny—the thought made her ill. Had he had a camera on them last night, to catch the moment so he could show his lawyer? She shuddered. How *could* she still love him?

Suzie wrapped her arms around her. 'Where's the jerk staying and I'll give him an earful.'

'Thanks.' Meg wiped her eyes. 'But I don't think that will help.'

'It couldn't hurt. Where's he staying?' Suzie stood up and straightened out her singlet and shorts—not that much could go askew when they were plastered to her body. 'Come on. I'm your friend, trust me.'

It had been a long time since Meg had trusted anyone. She took a deep breath. She couldn't go on alone. She needed help. 'At the Carlton Crest, I think. But I can do this on my own, Suz, truly I can. I'm managing fine.'

'Yeah, I can see that.' Suzie tossed the bakery bag to Meg and stormed into the hallway. 'Make yourself a cup of tea, then get tidied up. You look like death warmed up.'

Meg heard Suzie wrench open the front door.

'And put some perfume on.'

Jake slammed down the phone. Work needed him. He wasn't getting anything done here. He felt as though he was making a bigger mess of Meg's life. He grabbed his suitcase out of the cupboard and started throwing clothes into it. Her life had been perfect before he'd turned up.

It was his problem, not hers, that he couldn't cope with the past.

The sharp rap at his door shot straight through him. 'Not now Vivian,' he called. She was becoming more and more keen to spend her spare time with him, and he felt like a heel for not telling her the whole story, but he couldn't bring himself to confess his stupidity to her. 'I'll meet you at breakfast.'

The knock was louder.

Jake strode to the door and yanked it open. 'I said... Suzie?'

Suzie stepped into his room, stabbing his chest with her finger. 'I want to know what gives you the right to come storming into my friend's life and upset her!'

'Nothing.' He stepped back. 'No right at all.'

Suzie looked taken aback for a moment. Then she looked at his bag. 'That's right. Skulk off back to whatever hole you crawled out of and leave Megan alone.'

'That was the idea.'

She tipped her head and drew her eyebrows together, her whole bearing changing as her anger presumably gave way to curiosity. 'Why?'

'Because I'm making her life worse by being here.'

She stared at him, one of her finely arched eyebrows rising. 'You love her!'

He shook his head and held the doorknob even tighter.

'Yes, you do. Have you told her? She deserves to know.'

Jake looked up. She was right. He wasn't sure what love was any more, but the least he could do was tell her he was leaving. If he didn't he'd be as bad as she was, running away—and there was no way he was going to let her be haunted in the same way he had.

Admitting defeat sat like a twenty-ton 'dozer in the pit of his gut. He desperately wanted to tell Meg that both Dan's and his mother's accusations were pure fabrication, but...how could that make anything right for her now?

He had no other choice but to leave.

'It's too late.' His voice grated harshly. He'd put them both through enough. They might have been great together, but hanging onto the past was killing him—and Meg.

'It's never too late to fight for who you love.'

'And who is it exactly that you love, Jacob Adams?' Vivian stood resplendent at the door in a white suit. 'And *who* is this woman?'

He took the easy question. 'This is Suzie—' He had no idea what her surname was, and it looked as if she wasn't going to offer it. She was eyeing Vivian like a predator. She shifted her weight onto her heels and Jake half expected her to start pawing the ground. 'Meg's friend.'

'And what the hell is she doing *here*?' Vivian's shrill tone pierced through him like a knife as she swept into his room. She faced Suzie without flinching.

That was a good question. Defending Meg, he guessed. An odd wave of regret made him think it should be *him* defending Meg, not this slight woman with the fierce tongue.

'I came to invite Jake to Meg's for breakfast.'

'Why would you want to go?' Vivian stuck her dainty hands on her hips and glared at him. 'And why is it that everyone can call you Jake except me?'

Jake could see Vivian's temperature rising. Her cheeks wore slashes of red, far darker than the make-up she'd put on, and her eyes were several shades darker, giving him fair warning of a fierce storm brewing. Why? He couldn't fathom. Their arrangement was clear...unless this was improvisation on her part—part of the act.

'It was my name when I was a kid—nothing special.' Jake grabbed his coat. He didn't have time to explain what was going on to Vivian; he wasn't even sure himself. All he knew was he had to talk to his wife.

He didn't care what was running through Suzie's mind at Vivian's performance. It didn't matter. All that mattered was that she was tossing him a line, a chance to make it right with Meg. Where that would lead, he had no idea— and he hated that. He wanted to know exactly where every action led. He hated taking chances—especially with Meg's happiness.

'Well, I'm not being left behind.' Vivian moved close to him and looped her arm into his possessively. 'Where my *Jacob* goes, so do I.'

Jake snapped his attention to her. He wasn't hers by a long shot, and making claim to him in front of Meg's friend was about as tasteful as a stripper at a tea party, but Vivian didn't know any better. 'That may not be a good idea.'

'You're not going without me,' Vivian bit out, sauntering to the door. 'You may need me.'

She was right. He might. He prayed he wouldn't. He wanted it to work out this time. 'Vivian…' Jake softened his tone. 'I need to talk to you. It's important.' He didn't want her to go rushing in to Meg's with no idea of the truth.

'Later, honey,' Vivian purred, slinking through the door and into the hallway. 'I don't care—I'm coming.'

Jake had to hand it to Vivian. She was one hell of an actress. She almost had him believing they were an item!

Suzie shrugged. 'Fine. Come on, then. I'm sure Jake has nothing to hide.'

That wasn't quite true. Jake swallowed the lump of guilt rising in his throat. His good intentions were going to come back and haunt him and there was nothing he could do about it.

CHAPTER NINE

MEG wasn't sure what she was doing. Already her body was strung taut, ready to snap. She had no idea whether it was a good thing that Suzie had gone tearing off to drag Jake back to talk about their son or not. What if he refused, or she brought back worse news? What if he loathed her and couldn't stand to look at this witch who'd kept his baby a secret from him? Or what if he was playing uninterested while his lawyers worked overtime on the paperwork to take Tommy from her?

There was so much fear and indecision that she could hardly breathe. She'd had a quick shower and brushed life into her hair before pulling every item in her wardrobe out, much to Tommy's interest, in search of the right outfit. She didn't want to look desperate, or pleading, or weak, but she didn't want it to look as though she was trying too hard either. She settled on a pair of blue jeans and a cinnamon cotton shirt. She liked the casual but together look. She put on matching socks, which was a feat in itself, seeing as a black hole usually swallowed a couple of her socks every wash-day.

She had just fed Tommy breakfast and put him in the playpen in the lounge room when she heard a noise on the front step, followed by the doorbell.

Meg took several deep breaths, slapped her cheeks for colour—because she was sure all her blood had sunk to her toes—and forced herself into motion.

Maybe she could tell him to come back later, after she'd had time to write down and rehearse what the hell she wanted to say to the guy who'd cheated on her, who'd probably tricked her into a false marriage and who'd taken to drinking rather than living. She chewed on her lip. She knew for sure that he'd tricked her.

She swung open the door, a dozen expletives poised on her tongue.

A man stood on her stoop, facing the other way, his solid frame rigid as he looked both up and down the street, then up again. He must have heard the door open. Cautious hazel eyes met hers.

'What are you doing, Danny?'

'Can I come in?' He looked down the street again, turning his head to reveal a bruise on his cheekbone, all deep purples and blues.

'No.' The last thing she wanted was to invite trouble into her home.

'Please. I have to talk to you.'

'Is this about Jake?'

'Yes.' He touched his fingers gingerly to the black and blue mark.

'Then we have nothing to talk about.' Meg's mind churned with indignation, and she grabbed the door and started to close it. She paused, watching his pain as he touched the wound. 'Did he give you that?'

'Yes.' His deep voice wavered. He shoved his hands into his pockets and for all the world looked like a young teenager again. All shyness and insecurity. 'I need to talk to you.'

A swell of memories and feelings rushed over her and she couldn't bring herself to deny Danny, once her friend, anything. Meg let go of the door and it swung wide of its own accord. Danny slipped past her.

Meg eyed the discolouration on his clean shaven jaw and couldn't help but be curious as to why Jake would actually punch his best mate— Especially after setting them up, so he wouldn't have to pay out so much money for Tommy.

Her blood heated. She'd get this over and done with once and for all. 'Kitchen—straight down the hall.' Meg could use a cup of tea. A strong one with enough kick in it to give her the energy she needed to cope with this on top of everything else.

Meg grabbed the kettle. She felt as if she hadn't had a stiff cuppa for eons as she filled it. Her eyes darted out of the window to the three square metres of overgrown garden and lawn in the back yard. She hadn't had time for that either. 'Why did he do that to you?'

'I thought you could tell me.'

'Me—why?' She switched the kettle on and tried to look busy wiping down the laminated benchtop. She ran the cloth over the tiny black tiles on the wall as well—anything to avoid looking at Danny, his shiner and his preying eyes.

Meg's attention rested on the paper bag Suzie had brought, sitting on her petite round kitchen table. She opened it and set to arranging the warm flaky croissants she found inside onto a plate. By the time she'd finished more of the croissants seemed to be flaked and fallen in the bottom of the bag, over the bench and on her timber floor rather than on the plate itself.

Danny shuffled around. 'Because he said it was for you.'

'Oh?' Meg couldn't find the words. What the hell was going on? 'I don't know why he would've done that to you.' She met Danny's soulful eyes and couldn't help wondering how far Jake would go to get out of speaking about Tommy.

Danny shrugged, a sheepish grin tugging at his mouth. 'I guess it sunk in that I fancied you.' He ran his eyes over her as if he were assessing her for a job.

Meg wanted to scream! She'd thought *that* was the whole point! To get her besotted with Danny! An extreme charade to get her and her son off Jake's hands and into someone else's! The shiner might even be a prop to exact her sympathy. 'I didn't breathe a word to Jake of what you said to me last night, so I don't know what gave him that idea.'

Danny's face dropped. 'I think I do.'

'And why would that be, Danny?' She eyed him carefully. He didn't seem like the sort of guy who would deceive her because he was told to. Meg shook her head, trying to clear a way for logical thought. Was it a game, or all horribly real?

'Because I told him I loved you.'

'You love me?' Her voice caught in her throat. *Keep calm.* It can't be. Not Danny. Not love.

He looked sheepish. 'God, Meg. You're beautiful. Always have been. But you haven't looked past Jake at me, not once. I know I'm not much to look at, but I had hoped you'd eventually see me as someone more than just your friend.'

She rubbed her hands together, willing sensation back into her body. 'I'm sorry, Danny. I know you said you liked me last night, but I didn't really think...' If it wasn't a set-up then perhaps Jake had given Danny the shiner because he thought Danny *had* propositioned her.

Her mind tussled with facts, dates, conversations. She snapped her eyes to his face. 'You told Jake you loved me—when?'

'Three years ago. After you left. I figured it couldn't do any harm. And I was so sick of waiting around for him to come home and look after you properly.'

'Me too,' she whispered. Meg turned to the bench and attacked the cupboard for cups, her throat aching for all the years they'd lost. No wonder Jake had thought there'd been something between her and Danny.

Danny came up right behind her and wrapped his arms around her waist.

Meg turned, putting her hands over his so they didn't wander. She had the impulse to wrench them off, but this guy *had* been a friend, a good friend, despite everything. 'I'm flattered, Danny, but as I said last night—I'm not in love with you. You're a friend, that's all.'

She swallowed a wave of nausea. Danny might be the reason why Jake had never followed her, never found her. 'What you told me—about Jake with other women, and the booze…?'

The front door flew open.

Her gaze darted down the hall to the cause. Suzie, Jake and Vivian walked into the hallway.

Meg pushed Danny's hands away from her and jumped as far from him as humanly possible, her cheeks flooding with heat.

She dropped her gaze. She didn't want to meet Jake's prying eyes as he strode up the hall. She didn't owe him anything, least of all an explanation for this. He had Vivian, after all.

'Make yourselves comfortable in here.' Suzie swung her arm to the lounge room as if she was a show host. 'I'll just get the kettle on and help Meg.'

Meg glanced up and caught Jake's stony look. She felt stifled, and that Danny was still too close. She stepped a little further away from him, pressing herself hard against the bench to try and lessen the guilty pounding in her veins.

'I'll be happy to help you in here.' Danny took out the teapot and placed it on one of the large hand-painted timber trays that Meg had picked up at a market. 'I don't have to join them just yet.'

Meg could see the concern on Danny's face, written in ashen white with a dash of black and blue on the side. She'd rather hide in the kitchen too, than face those two. What an earth had happened to the idea of a quiet chat with Jake to sort things out? Nothing could be sorted, let alone discussed, with Vivian around.

Suzie rushed into the kitchen, took the barely boiling kettle and sloshed the contents into the pot, adding tea leaves as an after-thought. She shrugged when she saw that both Meg and Danny were watching, open-mouthed. 'No one's going to notice.' She bent closer to Meg. 'What's with you and this guy?' She tossed an assessing glance over at Danny.

'Nothing.'

'That's not what it looked like.' Suzie's eyes glowed with the intrigue and excitement of it all. 'Jake didn't miss it.'

Danny managed to turn another shade lighter at Suzie's words, whispered too loudly to be missed. Meg knew how he felt, but didn't know why. She didn't have to answer to Jake. She was her own woman.

Suzie pushed Meg towards the doorway. 'Get in there. I'll come in with the tea in a minute.' Suzie eyed Danny, who was opening cupboard doors in an effort to look suitably busy. 'I'm sure Danny here will help me.'

'Yeah.' He stood up and straightened, sounding pleased to be staying out of the way—especially of Jake and his long arms and formidable fists, Meg guessed.

Meg wanted to stay too. She'd only caught the slightest glimpse of Vivian and she looked incredible in a suit. Suddenly her casual look, that had appeared so perfect earlier, alone in front of the mirror, felt positively homely.

'What a quaint place you have here,' Vivian tittered as Meg stepped into the room. It looked as if she wanted to be anywhere but here by the way she'd perched herself on as little of the arm of the couch as she could.

'Thank you.' Meg tried to concentrate on how Tommy was faring with all these strangers. Thankfully he seemed blissfully engaged in his toy train, making a funny shooshing sound as he pushed it around him.

'I expected you to be doing better than this.'

Meg gritted her teeth, but she wouldn't even waste her breath explaining the costs involved in designing clothes to this woman.

Meg didn't want to look at Jake, but her eyes were drawn to him, slumped onto her couch. With a pang she realised he was doing his best to avoid her too—and succeeding. He wore a pair of grey trousers that looked as if they'd been left in a suitcase too long, and a cream shirt that screamed 'Pierre Cardin'. His hair appeared to have that 'I lost the comb and used my hands' look, and his jaw sported a shadow that was a good twelve hours old. Even tired he looked handsome, igniting memories. But he wasn't looking at *her*.

She tried to disguise her disappointment by diligently clearing the coffee table of fashion magazines, her sketches and doodles, a fluffy rabbit and an unwatched cartoon video. It had looked perfectly reasonable to have them sitting there before, when she'd perused the room for its tidiness, but now they signified the difference between Vivian and herself with such clarity that Meg felt her hands fumble—the homely housewife versus the sophisticate.

'I didn't know you had a child.' Vivian cast a wary glance at Tommy in the playpen, then at Jake. Her eyes clouded as if her mind had miraculously kicked into gear and she bit down on her lip.

Jake looked busy scouring the ceiling.

'Here's the tea.' Suzie looked pointedly at Jake, who reluctantly met her accusing gaze. 'I don't hear much talking going on.' She placed the tray onto the coffee table and started unloading it. The croissants, some biscuits, yesterday's teacake and a dozen pieces of fruit. 'Not exactly breakfast, sorry. Think of it as breaking tea.'

Meg thought about breaking necks and sat down heavily on one of her lounge chairs, trying to look as relaxed as she could while concocting ways to murder a certain friend, an almost ex and a simpering super-brat.

Danny sneaked in with the teapot and cups on another tray. If he could have tiptoed in with his load or become invisible Meg guessed he would have. Anything to avoid getting noticed…

Jake's eyes darted directly to Danny, the venom in his glare enough to kill a man on the spot. A muscle quivered in Jake's jaw and it was hard to miss the way his hands clenched into tight balls.

Danny coughed. He probably felt Jake's murderous eyes on him. 'Here's the tea. Hope you like it.' He backed up, retreating as far from Jake as he could manage without ever actually looking at him. He knocked into the playpen and turned, noticing Tommy for the first time. 'Huh? There's a kid in here.' He looked at everyone wide-eyed. He locked on Suzie. 'Yours?'

Meg watched as Suzie shook her head, her brow creasing. She was probably wondering how she'd managed to miss that in the motormouth conversation she'd undoubtedly subjected him to whilst in the kitchen.

Danny looked at Vivian.

'Of course not, you idiot.' Vivian stood up and threw her shoulders back. 'Look at his dark hair.' She took two steps forward and crouched in front of Tommy—keeping a healthy distance, Meg guessed, in case he could projectile vomit. 'He's Meg's and yours.'

The shock of it hit Meg full force. She was stunned silent, her whole body and mind immobile as an onslaught of emotion racked her control. Jake had deliberately fed his girlfriend a lie!

Danny's eyes glazed over; his face became pale. 'Mine?' He shook himself, smiling away his daze. 'No way. I've never had a kid—especially not with—' His eyes locked onto Meg. 'Heck, I haven't even had...' His stunned look rested on Jake. He threw up his hands. 'I swear. I never touched her.'

Meg covered her mouth with her hand, stifling the rush of obscenities that she wanted to hurl at them all. Of course Tommy wasn't Danny's. She snapped her attention to Jake. Why didn't he say anything? He sat immobile on the couch, his face stony and guarded.

'Oh, come on, Danny boy,' Vivian sneered. 'He's even got your eyes. They're as green as emeralds.'

Jake's blood chilled. His eyes were drawn to the little boy's—vivid green? His body stiffened; his heart thundered. His gaze glued to Meg, scouring her face for the truth. He couldn't miss the raw hurt that glittered there.

'Danny hasn't even got green eyes,' Suzie said, hands flourishing towards the little guy as if she was on a game show, presenting prizes. 'He's Jake's.'

CHAPTER TEN

JAKE leapt to his feet. Tommy was *his*? Joy bubbled up from his singing heart. A son. His own boy. And with Meg.

He saw her icy glare cutting into him, into his very core. A new anguish seared his heart. This little guy was a child that Meg had carried and borne without him because his mother and Dan had fed her a pack of lies. And what had *he* done, dragging Dan back and trying to get them together, shunning the boy and ignoring Meg's pleas for discussion?

What had Dan done? He snapped his eyes to him. It looked as if Dan had a fair idea, as he sank as pale as lime powder into the nearest chair. He was shaking his head—and well he might. His bruise showed up even more coloured against his pasty skin.

Jake had the uncontrollable urge to punch him again, just for the confusion and pain his so-called 'mate' had caused them both.

Jake's breath stuck in his chest. Maybe he was jumping to conclusions again. He needed Meg to say the baby was his, to tell him exactly.

'Mine?' His voice barely worked at all. 'But you said…'

Meg's face was bleak and her lower lip trembled.

Jake wanted to pull her into his arms but was welded to the floor by the naked hurt that lay in her eyes. And he was responsible for it.

'Of course he's yours, you idiot.' Suzie threw her hands on her hips and shot him a look of pure exasperation.

Jake cringed. He hadn't let Meg finish telling him that first night about the baby. What an idiot he was. He'd been so sure the kid was Dan's he hadn't given her a chance to finish, had been hell-bent on interrupting her every time the subject of the little guy had been mentioned since. He was a fool!

'Yours?' Vivian's voice hit a high note. 'You said there was nothing between you two. And she said—' She threw an accusatory finger at Meg. 'You said he was just the boy next door.'

'But Dan...' Jake couldn't even concoct a sentence. Meg was glaring at him, her cheeks flushed, her hands clenched into fists. He wished she'd punch him, pound him until there was no hate for him left. He couldn't keep going if she hated him.

'It's not mine, mate.' Dan edged towards the door and froze. 'Oh hell, Jake. What have you done?'

Jake glared at him. If Dan hadn't shot his mouth off about Meg all those years ago he wouldn't be sitting here now, looking like the biggest idiot, in this room charged with tension. He'd be coiled up in bed with Meg and his own son, happily married.

Dan must have been thinking the same thing. 'Cripes, I'm sorry, mate. I never meant for you to think that I... We didn't. Not a kid, Jake. I just felt so left out of your life, out of what you two shared.'

Jake raked his fingers through his hair. The boy wasn't Dan's. *He was his!* A warmth spread through him as quickly as it was followed by icy dread. What must Meg think of him now? He'd all but spurned the little fellow.

'What's going on?' Vivian demanded. 'Tell me this child is not yours, Jacob.'

Vivian's acting slid over him. 'Meg?' His voice was shaky.

She looked at him, her cold stare boring holes into him. 'Of course he's yours.' She touched her belly protectively, as if she was recalling the pregnancy, her eyes alive and glistening with unspoken pain.

Every muscle in his body tensed. What the hell could he do now? He'd mucked everything up, totally. He felt as if he was twenty paces back from square one. He was due in Brisbane at seven in the morning for a meeting with his consultants, with the very real risk of being in breach of contract if he didn't show. He couldn't lose his business now, not with a wife and son to look after. Whether they wanted him or not.

'Whose did you think he was?' Meg spat out the words as though she'd suddenly burst. 'Danny's! That's great, that is. You thought he'd— You thought I'd—' Fury seemed to choke her.

Suzie stepped forward, waving her hands around the place as if she could dampen the intensity of the anger in the room. 'It's okay. Just a misunderstanding. Communication is always a little difficult between the sexes. Like all that Venus and Mars stuff everyone keeps going on about.' She gave them each a warm look. 'Obviously some wires got crossed somewhere.'

Jake watched Meg gape at Suzie, then turn her attention to Dan. You would have thought he was a giant slug with ooze and stench pouring off him by the way she screwed up her nose and wrinkled her brow.

Jake felt a small buzz of satisfaction hum through him. Meg didn't love Dan. And it wasn't Dan's child. Tommy was *his* child. He looked at the little guy in the playpen, at the small hand, at the tiny thumb stuck in his mouth and the face pressed against the wooden frame, his eyes wide with concern. How was he going to convince Meg that the best place for her was back in his arms and under his roof?

Vivian zeroed in on Meg. 'Let me get this straight. First the infant is Dan's—now it's Jacob's? It sounds to me like you're some desperado, out to land whichever jerk believes you. Well, my Jacob is not going to fall into your trap.'

Jake was over by Vivian's side in a heartbeat, taking her arm, steering her into the hall and to the door. He stepped into the open air and breathed deeply.

'Tell me what's going on Jacob. I must know.' Vivian's voice wavered.

Jake ran his hand through his hair. 'Thanks, but this isn't the time for the act.'

'Who's acting?'

'Pardon?' She couldn't be for real. This was exactly what he didn't want happening. He'd mucked up enough lives to last him a lifetime.

'We've spent time together. I've enjoyed your company, Jacob. I hope you feel the same.' She rubbed a hand up his arm. 'I think we could have a future…'

Jake shook his head. He should never have brought her to Melbourne and into his past—his life. 'You're a great woman, Vivian, and you'll make someone a very happy man.'

'This sounds ominous.' She lowered her eyes. 'Is what Megan said *true*?'

'Yes.'

'But what about that Dan guy—did he ever make out with her?'

'No.' Jake thrust his hands deep into his pockets. How he could ever have believed the jerk in the first place was beyond him. Jealousy, he guessed, had fuelled Danny's jibes to explosive proportions over the years. 'The child's mine, Vivian. Really mine.' He wanted to howl and moan and celebrate all at once.

'First Danny and now you—is she a loose woman or just desperate to lay blame?' Vivian's voice was high-pitched and piercing.

'Neither. She's my wife.'

'Wife?' Vivian's make-up failed to cover the flush in her cheeks. 'You mean I've been helping you to get your wife back—the jealousy thing?' She stabbed him in his chest with one of her long nails.

'She left me three years ago. I owe it to myself and to her to talk things through.'

'And you obviously didn't know about the baby,' Vivian said more quietly. 'You assumed it was Dan's.' She paused for a moment in thought. 'She was pretty upset.'

'Yes, she was.' Jake had never seen Meg so upset, not even at her father's funeral. And it was killing him not to be with her, comforting her, explaining to her. But he had a responsibility to Vivian too, one that would only take another minute, while he'd take the rest of his life with Meg, if she'd let him. 'We just need some time to sort things out.'

'Fine,' she said haughtily. 'But you're still paying for my dress.' She let a small smile touch her lips. 'And you have to promise me something...that if it doesn't work out with you two my door is the first one you come knocking on.'

'Sure.' He gave her a gentle hug and a kiss on the cheek. 'Thanks.'

Jake stood with her on the front step until the taxi she'd called from her mobile turned up. The silence was awkward and Jake found himself straining to hear what was going on in the house. What did Megan think of him for presuming the child was Dan's? Was there a chance of them getting back together, or was he just deluding himself?

Jake walked back into the house determined to sort this all out, here and now. He'd get everything straightened out with Meg, then he'd catch the afternoon flight to Brisbane.

Suzie and Dan were sitting on the couch drinking tea and eating biscuits. His son was blowing raspberries as he swooped a large red plastic plane in the air. He felt a warm glow surge through him. He was a good-looking boy, and he'd bet really smart too.

'Where is she?' he demanded.

Suzie looked up. Dan turned green. 'In the kitchen.'

Jake strode down the hall. He could hear Meg was talking to someone and she wasn't happy. Her tone rose in pitch, then she fell silent, then strained words were uttered quietly, then silence. He came to the entry and faltered.

'I just need more time,' Meg said into the phone. She figured her day couldn't get any worse. 'Mr Bolton, I assure you I have an appointment at the bank tomorrow, and I'll get it all sorted out.'

'Ms James, I gather my aunt only called you last week. I specifically asked her to call you over two weeks ago. She has bills, debts, accounts that need to be attended to at the earliest convenience.'

'I understand. And I'm doing the best I can.' Meg threw back her shoulders and stood taller. 'You might like to keep in mind that I do have a contract with Mrs Bolton that clearly states the length of the loan period. And it isn't up. Nowhere near.'

'And I hope *you* understand, Ms James, that my aunt is sometimes overly generous with her money. I'm sure you will agree that when you entered into the contract you in no way and at no time wanted to disadvantage my aunt.'

'It doesn't help the situation for you to be calling me like this.' Meg took charge with a quiet assurance that she wished ran deeper. 'I understand the problem and am doing what I can to remedy the situation. These things take time.'

'You must be a busy woman.'

'Yes, very.' Meg remained calm despite her throat clogging up. She wasn't about to be intimidated. She'd survived so much already; she wasn't about to go down now. 'Actually, I'm in the middle of a very important meeting now.' She didn't care if he believed her or not. She wanted out of this conversation before she told him where he could stick the contract.

'I won't hold you up, then. Thank you for your time.'

Meg rang off. Yeah, right. He didn't care a hoot about her or her business, just his aunt's money matters. If only the dear old lady had called her earlier, as her nephew had suggested, Meg would've had time to sort all this out before Jake came crashing back into her life.

'Troubles?'

'Jake.' Meg turned. He leant against the wall. His hair was ruffled and dark shadows encircled his eyes. 'You look like death.' She hoped he was suffering as much as she was. 'What are you doing here? I thought you left?'

'It's time for us to get all this worked out.' His voice was smooth and insistent and it seemed unlikely that he would take any excuses.

'All what?' Her blood chilled. She didn't feel up to sorting anything else out. She'd had enough already.

'Everything. Are you in trouble, Meg?' His soft tone held concern and he moved closer.

'You tell me.' His musky cologne invaded her nostrils, sending frissons of awareness running rampant through her every nerve. She felt as if she was in trouble whenever he was around, worse when he was closer.

'Money trouble?'

She dropped her lashes quickly to hide her vulnerability. 'No, not at all,' she lied through her tightly clenched teeth, and turned away from him. There wasn't a chance in Hades that she'd admit her company's problems.

'I'd like to help you out.' He reduced the distance between them. 'I have money put aside—'

Meg cringed. 'No, thank you. I'll manage fine without your help.' She couldn't afford to give him one scrap of information or he might use it against her. Better to focus on Tommy. The last few moments flooded back to her. All her loneliness and confusion welded together in one surge of anger. She turned and slapped Jake across the face.

'What the—?' He worked his jaw and gingerly touched his stubbled cheek.

'That's for assuming I slept with Danny.' Her sense of loss was beyond tears, beyond anger, beyond her stinging hand that she rubbed against her thigh. Any hopes she'd had hidden in the recesses of her heart for them to have a happy ever after had been dashed the moment she'd realised he truly believed she'd slept with Danny.

'I'm sorry. I should have thought...' His voice was distant.

'Damn right you should have. As if I'd have made out with your best mate while you were away.' It was bad enough he was a womaniser, but for him to assume she was poured from the same adulterous mould fuelled her fury.

She saw a smile play in his eyes and she slapped him again.

'What was that for?' he asked indignantly, his stare drilling into her.

An oddly primitive warning sounded in her brain. 'I don't know. I just felt like it.' She swung away from him, afraid of what she might see in his eyes.

He grabbed her arm and pulled her roughly to him. His large hands took her face and held it gently and his look was so galvanising it sent a tremor through her.

Her flesh prickled at his touch and her heart took a perilous leap. 'What?' she demanded as harshly as she could while her body sang under his sensuous eyes. She needed to break his hold over her—or succumb to his charm again and lose everything she'd achieved.

'Meg.' Her name was a whisper on the air—charged, set, and ready to blow at any moment. He inhaled a deep breath and centred his gaze on her lips.

A hot ache grew within her and spread up to her throat. 'So what happened to your lanky-legged girlfriend?' Meg was barely able to keep her voice even. She knew he was weaving his magic over her and she wasn't about to let him succeed.

'She's gone,' he murmured, stroking her cheek with his thumb.

Meg's insides ached. 'That was easy. Disposable women. Disposable marriage.'

'It wasn't like that, Meg.' Jake dragged in a deep breath. 'She wasn't really my fiancée, not even a girlfriend. She was a woman I met through work who agreed to come down and act the part.'

Meg closed her eyes. 'Why?'

'So you didn't think I was going to come in and take over. So you could get to know me again at your own pace. So you felt safe. I thought she would help.' He lifted her chin. 'So now what?'

Her heart thumped uncomfortably. 'Now you pay up and get out of my life,' Meg blurted, before she lost herself completely in his touch.

He dropped his hands from her as if she'd scalded him. 'That's all you want from me? Money?' His eyes, dark and stony, stabbed her like needles.

Meg kept her ground, refusing to flinch and retreat before him. 'There's nothing else you have that I want.' She kept her voice cold and exact, his infidelities firmly in mind.

'Our marriage meant nothing to you, then?' Bridled anger laced his tone, along with something else that was elusive.

She laughed bitterly. 'It meant the world to me, Jacob Adams, but I know exactly what it meant to you.' Just thinking of all the women he must have had shattered her. But that wasn't the worst of it.

Jake's eyes darkened and a shadow passed over his face. 'What did it mean to me, then?'

Meg took a breath, stilling her pounding heart. 'I know you only married me because...' Tears stung her eyes as the words that had burnt within her for three years surged from her. 'Because you promised my father.'

'Who told you that?' Jake's voice was cold, exact, all emotion drained from it and from his face.

'Danny.' Meg swallowed with difficulty and found her voice. 'Danny told me, just after you left for your job. I was complaining about your lack of commitment to me and he told me.' Biting her lip, she looked away.

Jake stiffened. 'Danny isn't a reliable source.'

Her mind was a crazy mixture of hope and fear. Maybe there was a chance. Her heart lightened and she stared up into his face. 'Okay. You tell me the truth. Did you or did you not make a promise to my father?'

CHAPTER ELEVEN

THERE was a long, brittle silence. Long enough for Meg to regret the question and long enough for her to dread the answer.

Jake let out an audible breath. 'Yes.'

She shuddered inwardly. 'Then that's it.' Meg swung on her heel and stalked away from him to the far side of the kitchen. This was the end of them. 'Get out of my house.'

A tense silence enveloped the room. Meg couldn't look at Jake. The pulsing knot in her chest was threatening her composure. She shut her eyes and willed him to leave.

She heard his footsteps heading down the hall.

It seemed for ever before she heard the front door open and close. Her strength left her and she sagged onto the bench, draped her arms over the laminate and dropped her head onto them, tears biting at her eyes.

Meg heard Tommy's gurgles in the next room, glad that Suzie was keeping her distance, and her tongue, which was unusual for her. She'd expected her friend to burst in seconds after Jake had left to inspect the damage and give advice.

Meg crashed some dishes around in the sink. She figured if she was too quiet for too long Suzie would come in anyway, to see if she'd done herself in or whether she'd been murdered.

'I'm going now.' Danny's voice was strained.

'Bye.' Meg didn't want to see him out. She wouldn't mind if she never saw Danny again. What he'd done to her and Jake was unforgivable—there was no excuse for his lies. If he'd really loved her he would've wanted her to be happy...

She pulled another plate into the sink. The sooner Jake brought the divorce papers the better. Meg wanted to get this phase of her life over. A queasy hollowness stopped her train of thought. What would life be like without Jake? Like the last three years…empty.

She threw the last dish onto the drainer, breaking it. Suzie still hadn't shown up. Meg bit her lip and wiped her hands on her apron. A bit of space to get herself together was acceptable; thirty minutes of nothing—not a peep—was too much to swallow from Suzie if she was truly her friend.

Meg stomped into the lounge, ready to pour out a stream of rules pertaining to friendship, but her feet ceased to move. Her heart leapt to her throat. Suzie wasn't there, only Jake, on the floor playing trains with Tommy.

Meg shoved down the insane stirring of warmth she felt at the sight of them both on the floor together. Like two little boys playing innocently. Only Jake wasn't little, or innocent.

They both looked up at her. Jake's eyes were shimmering in the light from the window and Tommy's with delight. Jake's mouth was curved into an unconscious smile that quickly lost all shape as he assessed her stance and mood.

She forced remote dignity and pride into her voice. 'What are you doing here? I told you to get out of my house.'

'I was going to, but I wanted to meet Tommy properly.'

She shook her head—he was up to something. She could see it in his clouded eyes. He had a purpose and she was in trouble if he was going to use Tommy—she'd be helpless. 'So...now you have. Get out.'

Tommy stared up at her with wide eyes, his bottom lip quivering, his mind probably trying to decide whether to go with tears or another game of trains. He lifted a train to show Meg.

Meg nodded to Tommy and smiled, sending as much reassurance as she could muster to him. He didn't need to be upset on her account. She was upset enough for both of them.

Jake turned and smiled at his son. 'He's the most gorgeous little guy I've ever seen.' There was a tinge of wonder in his voice that warmed Meg's heart.

A tear ran unbidden down her cheek and she swiped it away with the back of her hand. 'I bet you haven't seen many kids.'

'No. I don't run in those circles.' Jake swung back to her. 'But I figure he'd be the best.'

Her body lurched at the heart-rending tenderness in his eyes. Blood drummed in her ears, a shiver of awareness coursed her entire body, and she had to lower her eyes before he saw how he affected her.

Some of her anger evaporated, leaving only confusion. 'And why's that? Because he's your son?'

'Because he's yours *and* mine, Meg.'

Meg took a deep calming breath. The last thing she needed was a sympathetic husband on her hands. 'Jake, I want you to leave.'

'I want to talk.'

'I'm through talking today.' She tried to sound tough and hard, but the day was wearing her down, as was his magnetism. A small mass couldn't hold out against the gravitational forces of a large charismatic body like Jake's for ever, and Meg wasn't sure how long she could stay on course.

'I'll help you clean up.' He stood up and pushed his hands deep in his pockets, surveying the crumby coffee table, the cups, and the empty plate with a biscuit trail across the floor to where Tommy happily played. No guessing who was the cookie monster.

'You—clean? Yeah, sure,' Meg jeered. 'Where's Suzie?' She could do with an ally fighting on her side. She needed reinforcements, fresh troops and supplies before she battled Jake again.

'She left.'

'Why?' She was alone in the house with Jacob Adams, except for Tommy, who wouldn't be able to read her signals and extract her from a bind if his future depended on it. Which it did.

'Because I told her to go and she figured it was a good idea.' His voice held depth and authority, as if he wouldn't even consider someone not doing as he suggested. 'Clever lady.'

Meg's head started to ache. 'You have to go. There's nothing to say.'

'What about Tommy?'

'What?' Meg had visions of him demanding custody, dragging her off to court, of visitation rights, of his mother parading Tommy in front of her multitude of friends like some new dress she'd acquired.

'Child support?'

She exhaled sharply. 'Yes, fine.'

He studied her thoughtfully for a moment. 'How much?'

Meg turned away from him. 'Whatever you think is fair. It doesn't matter, Jake.' All that mattered was getting out of all this with her boy and her sanity.

'It does to me.' His voice was velvet-soft and insistent.

Her head snapped up. 'Really? Why do I have trouble accepting that?' Meg scoffed. Suddenly it all felt too contrived to be real. He had presumed Tommy was Dan's, for goodness' sake. What the heck was she even talking to him for?

Jake cocked his head and offered her a small smile. 'Because of all the lies flying round the place?'

'Lies? *Yours*, I presume?' She cast him what she hoped was a withering glare.

'And Danny's. There weren't any other girls. And sure, I drank. But not that much. Heck, when you're out in the outback it's so bloody hot and there's so little to do when you're not working. Drinking is *the* pastime— and, no, I'm not an alcoholic, Meg.'

'It doesn't matter what you say, Jake,' she said quietly. 'The promise to my dad takes the cake.'

He shrugged and strode towards her, stopping just before his big strong body touched hers. 'You're right.'

Meg tried to throttle the annoying current of excitement racing through her veins at his proximity. She took a breath and looked at her feet, afraid that she might see the same desire in his eyes and be unable to stop herself. 'Please go.'

'Call me if you need anything,' he whispered, and kissed her on the forehead. There was sadness in his tone, and finality. She tried to catch a hint of what was behind the tone in his eyes, but Jake didn't look at her. He strode to the front door.

It was goodbye. Meg was sure of it. A pain in her chest made breathing difficult. Her throat ached, and her body was itching to stop him. There had to be something other than goodbye. Her feet followed him of their own accord, her eyes stinging mercilessly as tears threatened to spill over onto her cheeks.

The door closed behind him.

Jake was out of her life. She'd won. And she couldn't be more miserable.

CHAPTER TWELVE

JAKE leant against the wall and sank to his hallway floor, burying his face in his hands. He'd screwed his life up big time, and he'd taken Meg down too. He tore at the buttons of his sweat-soaked shirt, pulling it off and throwing it into a corner.

He couldn't stop thinking about her.

He cast a weary glance around his Brisbane base. It was efficient and tidy, neat and empty of anything worth having. Meg was over two thousand kilometres away, and he didn't even know Tommy. He wanted to know his own son.

He hated having to walk away from Meg.

He'd married her because he'd wanted her so badly that it had made him hurt in places no woman had ever touched. And there had been no doubt she *was* a woman on his return after the death of her father. At twenty-one she'd had every curve, every look, and a smile to melt him into a mass of putty at her feet.

It hadn't seemed to matter at the time that it was the big 'M' word he'd vowed from the start he wouldn't embark upon. He'd forgotten everything with Meg except that it was the best way to look after her—like her dad had wanted him to, like he wanted to.

Jake kicked off his workboots and rubbed the stubble on his jaw. He was going to get Meg back. It was just a matter of time.

He wished she'd accepted his offer to help her out of trouble. It would have been some consolation. Some small thing for him to share with her. But then that was probably the point of her refusing. She didn't want him as part of her life at all.

Jake stood up and went to the full windows, staring out across the city centre. It was a great view at night, but it was a grey jungle now, standing stagnant in the vile humidity of the late-January sun.

He was covered in sweat and dust and des-perately needed a shower. He'd spent all day on site, and had talked his way out of trouble with the consultants by promising the impossible in the next fortnight. He'd have to run the guys and the gear overtime and for all hours to get the work done. He looked at the cordless phone lying on a chair—he had about a million calls to make but only one number that he wanted to dial.

The phone rang.

Jake snatched it up. It could be Meg. Or work. Anything for a distraction. And work was the best distraction of all against the gnawing ache in his chest.

'Jacob, I just got the dress. It's magnificent.' Vivian's voice was unmistakable, as was her tone. 'I wondered whether you'd changed your mind and would like to see me in it at the charity gala.'

Jake rubbed his neck and dropped onto the chair. 'Sorry, Vivian,' he said simply. What else could he say? It might not have worked out with Meg yet, but he wasn't going to give up.

'Actually, I'm glad. I've got this lovely gentleman begging to take me. But I thought I'd better make sure of you first.' She faltered, obviously floundering. 'I'm not angry, you know. And just to show you what a good sport I am—' Vivian tittered '—I'll tell you...I showed off my dress to my mother's friends and they simply died when I told them who made it for me. Megan J has plenty of fans, and if she can get some proper backers and get her designs into production she'll do really well.'

Jake knew first hand that backers didn't grow on trees. He'd gone all out to find a partner to ease the burden of starting his business but hadn't found one with enough confidence to do it. He'd ended up on his own, starting on small drainage jobs, putting everything back into buying more gear until he had a small but efficient company that he could talk into tenders for subdivisions. And now they'd won a million-dollar tender he had to build the thing—and he was darned if he was going to

muck up his first big chance with the consultants.

He straightened. *If he could find some
backers for Meg...*

'How's it going with you two? Is she there
with you?'

'Not yet.' Jake was short. 'I'll tell her you
liked the dress.' It would give him a good excuse to talk to her. That and the lure of backers
in Brisbane. *If* he could get her up here...

'Actually, don't mention me to her.' Vivian
lowered her voice. 'It wouldn't go down at all
well.'

'Why's that?'

'Just trust me on this one. Jealousy is a
funny thing. Hard to admit to but impossible
to ignore.'

'But Megan wouldn't be jealous.' Jake's gut
warmed. It would be incredible if she was; that
would mean he might have some claim on her
emotions. He threw out his chest and sat a little
taller.

'Why not? She's a red-blooded Aussie girl.'
Vivian laughed lightly. 'And I have to admit
that I have excellent taste in men.'

'Which means what?' He was cautious. It sounded as if Vivian was playing at something, but for the life of him he couldn't figure out what.

'That she probably loves you,' Vivian said. 'And if it's not love, it's lust.'

Jake smiled. Either one sounded good to him.

'What about your interview with the reporter?' Joyce volleyed. 'You've cancelled on him three times already!'

'Tomorrow. Make it tomorrow.' Meg slammed her office door and leant heavily on it. She was overworked, overstressed and out of her mind and body reliving her last hours with Jake over and over for the entire week.

She'd dragged herself to the bank, only to discover that the stuffed shirt she spoke to had decided she had neither the assets nor the cash-flow to take out a loan the size she required.

Joyce was successfully detouring and delaying Mrs Bolton's nephew's calls, so she had a chance to think of a solution, but she was having trouble getting ideas on how to have several hundred thousand dollars drop in her lap from the sky. She'd bought a lotto ticket in desperation, but with no luck. Life just didn't seem to be on her side.

She was exhausted. Finished. She'd have to tell the girls to finish the dresses they were on and let them know to start looking for other jobs, then she'd go back to a loft operation. Where exactly the loft would be eluded her. Her terrace house, although it was wonderfully situated, close to the boutique and within walking distance during the daylight hours, didn't have a garage. If she found a clean, small room to rent she'd at least have the money to continue buying the bolts of satin and silks for the outfits.

She would be like the elves from the fairytale again—for nearly a year she'd made only enough to buy the fabric for another outfit plus one. Now it looked as if she was heading back to the once-upon-a-time scenario without ever getting to the happy-ever-after part.

She hated the thought of letting any of her girls go. They were like a big family—although sometimes she felt a little bit left out being the boss, the slave-driver, the flogger. She shook her head. The girls must have sensed what was up by now—the mood around the place was positively chilly.

A man coughed.

Meg flung herself off the door and spun on her heel.

Jake sat on the couch. His blue jeans and polo shirt did nothing to detract from his air of authority and power. Casual never looked casual on Jake. His hair was neatly cut and combed and his face was cleanshaven. Meg flexed her fingers, resisting the urge to step forward and run a hand along his jawline.

'What are you doing here?' She wasn't sure whether to be scared or go with the glow that caressed her insides. She'd felt like death warmed up the last week, worrying about Jake. Now, here was the man himself. No cape, but definitely still sporting the ability to reduce independent women to tears in a single week.

'Meg.' His voice was velvety, thick and heavy. His eyes raked over her and she felt the need to straighten her wild hair, that she'd been tossing left, right and back during the course of the morning. Her cream trouser suit still looked reasonable, despite the wrinkles from sitting too long in too many places.

'I've got a proposition for you.'

Her heart jumped to her throat; her pulse skipped a few too many beats. 'A what?' She stood there as if she were fused to the floor, blank, amazed, every muscle in her body succumbing to the trembles.

'You've gone pale, Meg. I didn't mean a personal one.' He paused, and by the glint in his eyes it looked as if he was considering the prospect and finding it an interesting idea. 'I meant a business proposition.'

With an odd twinge of disappointment she felt her body ease off in its intensity. Her temper rose in response. 'No way, Jake. I've already told you. I'm not taking your money.' She hesitated. 'For anything other than support payments for Tommy, and college for him, and maybe a helping hand when it comes to puberty.' She saw his blank expression. 'The birds and the bees,' she clarified.

Jake's eyes darkened and widened, but his tone remained light. 'Sounds like a bit of a large dose of responsibility you're throwing at me.'

Meg ignored the jibe. 'So? Don't you think you're up to it?'

'On the contrary, Meg, I feel at this time in my life responsibility is just what I need.' The set of his chin suggested he was in all earnest. He leaned forward, resting his elbows onto his knees, and eyed her warily.

Meg swallowed. She tried to figure out his motive. He had to be up to something. He always was. He loved a challenge, thrived on it. She hadn't been a challenge when she was young, when he was courting her, or when he'd married her, whereas work always had. Now she was sure she was slotted into his 'too hard' basket, which made her a prime target.

'I was talking to a few of my friends at the country club.' He spoke carefully, as if he was weighing up each word, ready to change tack if she showed the slightest reaction the wrong way.

'Like Vivian?' Meg blurted. She didn't care what game Jake was playing. She was going to say what she wanted, when she wanted, and to hell with the consequences. 'Did she get her dress? Did you get the bill?'

It had been like closure, or as near to it as she figured she'd get, when she'd packed up the emerald satin gown herself and given it to the courier—as if she'd been closing a door on a chapter of her life.

He tilted his brow and looked at her uncertainly. 'Yes. She got her dress, and was absolutely thrilled, and I got the bill. But, no, it's other associates that are interested in investing in your label.'

Meg's spirits brightened. 'Really? You're not kidding?' Her brain leapt into action. 'You didn't tell anyone about my trouble, did you, Jake?'

'Meg, it was nothing like that. I didn't have to say anything other than I knew you.' His eyes looked as if they remembered in what biblical sense as they ran down the length of her body. 'They were thinking more in line of getting a good investment. Are you interested?'

She tried to quell the surge of excitement swelling in her belly at his look, replacing it with curiosity and possible optimism at the prospect of more investors. Meg didn't want to rely on other people's money, or take anything, especially charity, from Jake, but it looked as though she had no choice if she wanted to save her business.

Meg should have guessed it would be someone else interested in investing in her label. 'Yes,' she managed without too much enthusiasm.

Jake rose from the sofa.

His body called to hers as he straightened. Tall, handsome, and beautifully proportioned. She'd once run her hands over it, kissed and known every inch so very well. 'I've got tickets on the four P.M. flight to Brisbane.' His mouth curved into a smile.

Her blood froze in her veins. How dared he assume she would agree to waltz off with him? 'But Tommy...?' She bit her lip. The bigger problem was spending serious time with Jake. Her heart skipped a beat. It was hard enough to stay in control of her traitorous emotions and body in short stints, let alone hours at a time. 'I could find investors here in Melbourne...' But she had no time left to look for her own—she'd have to take his or lose everything she'd worked for.

'Or you could see the ones ready to go in Brisbane.' His expression stilled and grew serious. 'Can you call your sitter and make arrangements?' Jake smoothed his jeans out as if they'd suddenly changed size on him, and checked his mobile phone's tenuous position on his belt.

The real question, Meg figured, was whether she'd want to go to all the trouble of arranging everything to put herself smack bang in a battle zone. She knew that the future of her business was at stake if she didn't get her personal life under control. She cast her eyes over

Jake's very tempting body and bit her lip. She would just have to manage. 'I'll give it a try.' Meg sat down at her desk and resolutely picked up her phone.

Jake walked across the room and reached for the door handle.

'Thanks.' She broke into a warm, friendly smile that she felt sparkled in her eyes as well as her heart. If she was going to struggle through the next day or two in his company she might as well not make it any easier for him than it was for her. Her smile widened. She would have him in cold showers at least three times a day just to get even for how good he looked.

Her smile brought an almost immediate softening to his features, his green eyes glinting, almost burning with a secret faraway look. 'I'll meet you at your place just before three.' He returned her smile, his so warm and sensuous that it sent waves of excitement crashing through her nervous system.

She lowered her eyes, fighting the swell in her chest. *She loved him.*

Meg shook off the thought. It was just her imagination, she told herself fiercely. At three she was definitely raising the subject of divorce again. That would sort out her aching, desperate body once and for all.

CHAPTER THIRTEEN

JAKE seemed to manage to ignore her on the flight, despite Meg's tight blue jeans and tank top. She hadn't deliberately chosen the skimpy top, but it was too hot for much else and she knew it would be even hotter in Brisbane.

Meg couldn't relax in her seat. She squirmed, wriggled and dropped her purse to the floor. She stared at it ruefully, irritated that she was reacting like a bumbling schoolgirl.

Jake didn't seem to notice.

Meg bit her lip and distracted herself by focusing on a youngster in the middle aisle who was giving his poor mother a hard time. She toyed with the headphones she'd picked up on her way out of the terminal, her sympathy going out to the woman who was whispering desperately to placate the child. Meg lunged over Jake to pass the headphones to her.

Meg's breasts brushed against Jake's chest and she couldn't miss the way he sucked in his breath and stiffened.

He moved suddenly.

He snatched the phones from her and thrust them at the boy, his arms much longer and more useful for the reach. One look at his compelling profile and she lost all sense of gravity. She slumped back into her seat.

Jake sat rigid and silent. Meg didn't move, couldn't speak. And they stayed that way throughout the flight. No matter what she thought up she couldn't utter a word into the heavy, tense silence hanging between them. She wished she hadn't surrendered her headphones—she could have done with some escape from Jake's very solid, tacit presence beside her.

It was a relief to grab her overnight bag at the carousel, apart from the fact that Jake was right beside her in the crush of people. He brushed his hot body against hers as he reached for his own bag and her blood heated at the contact, her mind rushing with memories, her skin yearning for his hands and lips.

Meg staggered backwards. She had to concede that she wasn't coping at all well in the control department, but then she hadn't been with any other men, while Jake, she was sure, had relieved his pent-up desires with whatever willing and available female came his way.

Meg pushed through the crowd into a less claustrophobic area. The air was cooler and she took a few deep breaths to calm her flustered body.

A hand gripped hers.

Her eyes darted up to Jake's compelling eyes that riveted her to the spot. She was vividly aware of the strength and warmth of his fingers interlaced with hers, but he no more than assessed her identity and state of readiness for departure before leading her out of the airport.

Damn him for being so calm and controlled. His hand sent waves of electricity scorching through her body, hell-bent on burning out every nerve on the way.

It only took Meg a minute to identify Jake's car as the twin-cab four-wheel drive sitting, high and shiny clean, amongst hundreds of low-slung sedans around it. She cast him a hooded look.

Jake glanced at her. 'Fine, you were right. I drive a four-wheel drive, just like your father did. Are you happy now?'

Meg shrugged and smiled inside. 'It's okay, Jake. You can drive whatever you want. It certainly is a practical vehicle in your line of work...'

Jake eyed her as he threw the bags in the back seat. She could see some of the tension loosen from his muscles but he didn't oblige her with conversation. He unlocked her door and swung it open for her, not waiting for her to climb in before he strode to the other side.

No more playing the gentleman? Did that mean that he was through playing games? Meg's neck muscles tightened. Or had he just changed the rules?

Meg fumbled with her seat belt, her hands unwilling to co-operate in being the cool calm businesswoman she liked to think she was.

Jake didn't even glance at her as he did his belt up and thrust the key into the ignition. The car roared to life. Jake shifted it into gear and cruised over to the boomed exit. He handed both the money and the car park docket to the attendant. The read-out stated ten hours.

'You came down just for me!' Meg's stomach fluttered. 'I thought you had other business in Melbourne that you were attending to. You could have rung me.'

'I didn't know whether you'd come.' He worked the clutch and shifted the car into gear again as the boom lifted, joining the stream of traffic heading to the main road.

Had he planned to strong-arm her into coming, no matter what? 'So what would you have done if I'd said no?'

Blackmail? Bribery? Torture? She let her mind run off on a tangent, filled with Jake's hands and what torture he could exact upon her more than willing body.

'Convince you.'

Meg wondered what on earth he could've said in person that he couldn't have said on the phone. She glanced at his hard thighs as they pumped the clutch, and his large long hands as he worked the gears, and knew exactly what he'd had in mind. He couldn't have used his sexual magnetism over the phone, whereas in person...she was a push-over. Again.

She gritted her teeth. But it was for the right reasons, she told herself. She'd have her well-structured life back the way she liked it, where she could spend nearly half her day with Tommy and the rest of the day carving out a future for them. 'Where are we staying?'

'At my place.'

She swallowed hard, lifted her chin and darted a very direct and honest stare of incredulity in Jake's direction. 'I don't think so. I think a hotel would be better.'

Jake swerved the car off the road, yanking the handbrake on and turning in his seat to face her. He tilted his head and probed her eyes. 'You're not scared of me, are you?' His eyes glittered with dark promise.

Damn right she was. And rightly so. She couldn't trust herself not to fall into his arms when every inch of her was aching for his touch.

'No.' She wasn't sure whether she wanted to sound convincing or not, and it made her scared of what she might do next, to complicate her life further.

'I'll be a perfect gentleman.' Jake steered the car back into the traffic.

Damn. Her body was screaming for attention. She had to think of something else. Focus on something else. Food seemed much safer for her sanity than the alternative. 'What about dinner?'

'I'd love to, but I've a mile of work to do and I figured baked beans on toast—hope you don't mind?' Jake cast her a glance. 'We could order a pizza if you're not into beans?'

'No worries. Whatever.' Meg lay back in the bucket seat, trying to ease the emotions raging within her. She'd been flat out since Jake's visit this morning—organising Tommy, the office, her appointments—including that pesky reporter—and packing. She closed her eyes and tried to relax, but she could hear Jake, feel Jake, smell Jake and it was driving her mad.

Meg clung to reality.

'How long do you think it will take me to have meetings with the potential investors?'

He stiffened. 'I thought we'd do it together.'

'Not a chance.' Meg darted him a careful glance. There was no way he was going to take control of her life! 'If you hadn't noticed, Jake Adams, I've managed pretty well without you. Thank you for your help in lining them up, but I'm quite capable of taking over from here.'

A muscle spasmed in his jaw. 'Fine. I figure all tomorrow, maybe half the next day. You don't need to worry; you'll be back on the plane Wednesday night.'

She wasn't sure if she should feel relieved or concerned. What was the reason behind his generosity—feelings of regret for the past, obligation to Tommy, or duty to her father's promise? Meg bit down on her lip. None of them were flattering.

Jake pulled the four-wheel drive over to a space at the kerb in a very nice neighbourhood of inner Brisbane. She had no idea where she was exactly—she'd been more intent on remaining in total control of her faculties than where she was—the trip had passed in a blur.

'This is it.' Jake tossed a finger in the direction of a four-storey copper-rendered building with an overkill of glass windows—all style and no character.

Meg opened her door and leapt out, taking deep calming breaths. She shivered and rubbed her arms despite the warm climate.

A body-warm jacket was draped over her shoulders and she felt Jake's hand brush her neck, sending a surge of awareness through her. She darted a look at him and was startled to see gentleness in his eyes.

'Thanks.' Meg wasn't sure whether to be glad of the coat or afraid of what lay behind the look in his eyes. There was no way there was a future with Jake. She wasn't a dope. She'd learnt her lesson the first time around.

Jake's place was like any other belonging to a man who lived alone and could afford a housekeeper to come in—neat, sterile and uncluttered. The black chairs, the black iron table with smoked glass top, the unlived-in feel struck Meg in the pit of her stomach. It was as though he spent more time away than at home…

Meg stood in the hallway next to a set of very muddy work-boots pushed to one side and a hall table with a black cordless phone. Jake dropped his keys onto the tray next to the phone and hustled Meg in further.

'Feeling reluctant?'

She could hear his amusement. 'No.' She stepped into the room as quickly and as boldly as in the days when he'd dared her to do crazy things to a chorus of chicken calls when she'd been young.

'This way.' He stepped to the first door on the left and swung it open. A large double bed decked out in black and cream stood in the centre of the room.

'Bit of a dark fetish?'

'Not really, just my mood when I bought the stuff.' Jake strode into the room and dumped her bag on the bed. 'There's an *en-suite* in there.'

'And you're sleeping…where?' She wished she could feel more relaxed about the whole arrangement, but the idea of Jake's hot pulsing body anywhere within a kilometre of her was almost too much to consider.

A rumble escaped him; his smile was contagious. 'In the next room. I promise you I won't come and invade your privacy unless you invite me to.'

Meg turned away. That was what she was afraid of.

She heard the door close behind her before she even realised Jake was leaving. She wanted to cry out for him, but quickly clamped down on the impulse. It was immature and primitive, to say the least, not to mention totally insane. Jake in her bed again, save for the pleasure, was only a masochistic fancy.

The ring of Jake's mobile and his muffled voice were enough to let Meg know that he was engaged elsewhere for the time being. She unpacked her things, then lay down on the bed and closed her eyes.

Meg awoke to the clatter of pans and rose groggily from the soft bed. She shook her head as she moved towards the door, hoping her hair had that sexy tousled look that normally took ten minutes with the hairdrier. She glanced at a mirror just as she grasped the door handle. Yikes! She spun on her heel and entered the *en-suite*, brushing her hair enthusiastically to rid it of that terrible bird's nest imitation it was prone to.

'Just in time.' Jake cast a brief glance in her direction and placed two plates of piping hot baked beans on toast onto the table. He'd changed into a white T-shirt that hugged his torso, close and clinging.

Meg sat down at one of the settings and Jake took the other. 'I'm starved.' Meg took a mouthful. 'You make a mean bean.'

He smiled. 'Straight from the can—I can do no wrong.'

She couldn't bear his smiling eyes and what they did to her body and mind. Meg turned her head to the lounge suite and coffee table, covered in what looked like construction drawings. 'Busy?' She nodded towards the large sheets of paper.

'Yes. Always.'

'Just the way you like it.' So he didn't have to face himself and his emotions. He was always on the run. From when she'd first met him he'd been on the go, dropping his football and leaping over her fence to see what was happening with the new arrivals. He had always been hyper, in an effort to outrun his own reality and his life.

Jake ignored her jibe. 'I do small industrial and residential subdivisions.'

'Working for someone?' Probably the biggest company in Australia, so he wouldn't have to stay on one job with the same crew day after day.

Jake put down his fork. 'No, I work for myself, Meg. I choose my own hours and make my own money.'

She didn't know what to say. Was he implying that things would have changed eventually? That it all would've been okay if she hadn't run out on him? But it would have been a lie. How could her father have made Jake make a promise like that?

The silence stretched on. Jake picked up another load of beans.

'I like your place.' Meg was determined not to let the silence take over this time. 'But what about our house? What did you do with it?' It was pretty obvious that he would have sold it. She must have severe masochistic tendencies to ask about it—to even be here.

Jake's fork froze mid-way to his mouth. 'You really want to know?' It was as though he was searching her face for honesty. 'I couldn't stay there on my own. I tried.'

Her stomach sank. She could imagine him selling up as quickly as possible, to rid himself of her and his obligation to her.

'You sold it.'

The hurt must have been in her voice. Jake leant over the table and clasped her hand in his warm one, curling his fingers around and squeezing gently.

'No.' His voice was deep. The warmth from his hand spread up her arm and into her heart. Meg looked up at him, her heart pounding a little faster. He'd kept it? She didn't have any idea what that meant. 'Are you renting it out?'

'No. A cleaner goes in once every couple of months.' His words seemed guarded, as though he might be opening himself up to a woman on the warpath for his assets.

'Oh?' Meg ignored the nagging sense that she was slipping into danger. 'Why didn't you just sell it?' She regretted her words as soon as they were out. She wasn't Suzie. She was used to prevaricating around the truth, not just demanding a straight answer. She found a sudden respect for Suzie's bravery. Meg didn't have the iron-clad nerve that Suzie did, and she was scared to death of the answer.

'I couldn't sell it, just in case. I sort of thought you would, you know...' He looked away from her, his voice thick. 'I thought you would come back.'

Meg's hand rested on his arm of its own accord, and the heat of him coursed along her veins. Her mind struggled with the conflicting emotions racing through her—excitement, lust, fear and guilt.

His vivid green eyes blazed into hers and all thought left her mind.

She didn't realise she'd moved, nor notice Jake move, but suddenly they were face to face, standing next to the table, the meal forgotten, hands entwined, staring into each other's eyes with a fierce heat that couldn't be ignored a moment longer.

Meg ached from the tip of her toes to the top of her head, and her mind clambered for control of the situation amidst the dizzying rush of desire.

She ran her tongue nervously along her dry lips and Jake's stormy eyes darted to them. Then his warm mouth was upon hers.

His lips were hard and searching, his tongue tracing the soft fullness of her mouth and sending shivers of lust running through her veins like lava, flowing hot, hungry and relentless.

Meg ran her hands up his back, feeling his muscles quiver beneath them. She wrenched his T-shirt free and slipped her hands underneath to touch his hot flesh. It was so good to touch him again. Dreams of him had haunted her, taunted her, with the magic she'd left behind.

His kiss deepened. He plundered her mouth and his hands ran down her back, up her sides and over the swell of her breasts. Her emotions whirled and skidded as his hands wove their enchantment.

He cupped her breasts, fondling them as he would delicate porcelain, and stroked his thumbs over the swell pushing against her bra. Meg's breasts surged at the intimacy of his touch.

He slipped the straps of her top down her shoulders and the fabric fell to the floor, her bra following. Meg couldn't hold back any longer. She brushed herself up against him.

Jake groaned and together they wrenched his shirt off in a flurry of hands and kisses. He wrapped his arms around her and gathered her close to his pounding heart, his chest heaving against her shoulders.

She drank in the comfort of his nearness. It had been too long. It was like the first time, yet not. She already knew his entire body, committed to memory and mourned for years. There wasn't the fear or the shyness, just the overwhelming need to reclaim every inch of him.

His lips seared a path down her neck and across her shoulder. Hot, fervent kisses, as though he was in a hurry to capture as much of her as he could before the moment came to an end. His work-roughened hands caressed her skin, imprinting her with his touch, his hands massaging her breasts to arousal, rolling her nipples between his fingers until they were hard and as hungry for his lips as the rest of her.

His mouth covered hers again, and Meg kissed him back with all the greed of three years of celibacy. She ran her tongue along the softness of his inner lip, taunting him with small movements of suggestiveness.

She trailed kisses across and up his jaw, to tantalise his lobe with her mouth and tongue, breathing into his ear until he moaned.

Jake swept her up into his arms and carried her purposefully to his bedroom, dropping her onto the black cotton sheets. He collapsed onto her, plundering her mouth with his with such expert tenderness and need that Meg couldn't help but claw at his clothes.

She ran a hand down the length of him and caressed the hardness of his desire.

Jake kicked off his jeans and purged her of her own in a rush of arms and legs, hands and cloth.

Naked.

Every inch of him seemed to be bronzed by the wind and sun. There was no doubt he spent most of his time on a shovel next to his men and a fair amount on the beach to even the tan. She ran a hand over his taut muscles and smiled at what wonders he was about to show her.

Jake sat back, drinking in the sight of her with his eyes.

Meg wanted to feel embarrassed about her stretch marks—white and long on her belly—but couldn't. Jake was looking at her as though she was perfect.

He lowered himself down next to her. Body against body. She could feel the length of him, the heat of him and his desire for her. He touched her stomach softly, tracing the scars with a finger, one at a time, a glistening warmth in his eyes.

'Meg...' His voice was deep and thick, laden with emotion. 'I...'

Meg reached up, slid her hand along his cheek, around his neck and pulled him down to her. Her lips brushed against his, banishing his words, his thoughts and any hesitation he might have had. She writhed beneath him, her nipples tingling against his hair-roughened chest. His tormented groan was a heady invitation.

She kissed him. His lips, gentler, softer, more adoring than demanding, worked their way along, down her chin and neck, as his hands moved magically over her breasts, along the length of her, down across her waist, down her thighs and up her back.

Jake kissed every nerve in her neck, her throbbing pulse, her bones, her muscles and every curve and hollow. His breath heated her blood to flaming temperatures, setting every part of her body on fire for his touch.

His lips moved down over her heaving breast and claimed a nipple with tantalising possessiveness, fondling it with his tongue, caressing her until she was driven wild. The other hand slid over her stomach to the swell of her hips, down her legs. His hand explored her thighs and then moved upward. He ran his fingers through her soft downy mound and deeper, into the folds. She quivered in anticipation.

His long sensual movements caressed her to molten honey, dipping into her to feel her moist heat then out again to feel her, rub her, stroke her until she was burning hot for him.

Jake's lips left her breasts and made a path over her ribs to her stomach, and lower, to where his hand had just been. His lips traced a sensuous path and his tongue excited her to spirals of ecstasy.

Jake finally reclaimed her mouth possessively, plying her lips with his.

He was going to take her, and she wanted him to, desperately needed him to—more than anything. But something inside rebelled. She twisted beneath him, pushing him back onto the soft covers. She wasn't going to be taken.

Passion pounded the blood through her heart, chest and head, making all thought impossible but the most primitive instinctual one. Mate. She mounted him. *She* was going to take *him*.

She welcomed him into her body, sliding him up and down within her until waves of ecstasy flowed through her. She guessed it had always felt this good with Jake, but she couldn't override the sense that this was the best ever.

Meg pressed her hands against him and twined her fingers into his chest hair, teasing and pulling as she moved. His eyes burnt dark and fiery as he lifted his hands to capture her breasts again.

When he sat up and covered her breasts with his mouth Meg felt he wanted to throw her on her back and take her, but he didn't. He tasted her, licked her, and fell back against the pillows as she drove down hard onto him.

He bucked his hips beneath her. 'Meg,' he groaned.

Her eager response matched his and their desire overrode everything else.

Shivers of delight reverberated through her, her whole being flooded with Jake. She collapsed on top of him.

Eventually she rolled to one side and closed her eyes. She was filled with an amazing sense of completeness.

Meg opened her eyes some time later to see Jake propped on one elbow and staring at her, his eyes gleaming devilishly bright. The implication sent waves of excitement racing through her.

'I hate you, you know,' she said lightly, running her hand down his chest.

He smiled, capturing her hand and turning it palm upward. He pressed his lips in the hollow. 'I know,' he said, his voice caressing her every nerve. 'Meg, I...'

Meg smothered his words with her lips. She didn't want to talk, to ruin the now with the past and the pains. She just wanted him. Again and again.

CHAPTER FOURTEEN

SHE was not a morning person. Meg moaned as she rolled over, colliding with a solid wall of hot flesh. Her mind kicked in and she recoiled. What had she done? She was here to make her life easier, not to create more complications!

'Hey?' Jake's voice rumbled through her, a hand sliding around her waist and holding her warm in his arms.

Meg hesitated only for a moment. His arms felt so good and strong, but there wasn't a future with Jake. Sure, the sex was terrific, but that was all there was. All there ever had been. A marriage needed more to make it work, and she wasn't about to make the same mistake again.

'I'm going to be late!' She rolled out of bed and away from Jake before he could move. 'I need extra time to get ready. I don't want to look like a sloth.'

She was out of the door and into her room before she heard Jake move. She had to get her head examined. She *knew* Jake was dangerous. She ran a hand through her tousled hair—she'd never expected herself to break on the first night.

She covered her mouth as reality dawned on her. They hadn't used protection! She closed the door firmly and leant heavily on it. Her life was a mess.

Meg opted to busy herself with getting showered and ready rather than think about the possibilities. She hadn't lied when she'd said she needed time to get ready. Getting herself composed again was going to take a while, especially since she'd left her sense behind in Melbourne.

Her body still sang from Jake's touch and her loins still burned hot for him. She could hear the water running next door and it was all she could do to convince herself to stay in her room—not go and help him get ready in the shower, together.

Jake would be naked. Her body buzzed at the thought, but she halted her feet's progress to the door and headed for the wardrobe instead, pulling out her cream two-piece suit.

She'd already done enough.

The investors' homes passed by in one glamorous blur of smiles and faces, handshakes and nods. It had gone well, Meg admitted. She'd apprised them of her current orders, the potential of cash flow, given the right advertising, and shown them two folders of photos of the designs themselves, on very curvaceous models from the last show.

The women had loved the clothes, the men the models—with several of them pledging her large chunks of money for a share in her label, available when the appropriate documents were drawn up and signed.

Jake wasn't as easy to get by with. He'd turned up at her last appointment of the day to save her a taxi ride back to his place. But he wasn't stupid. He knew she wasn't falling over backwards or jumping on him in the car, like in the old days.

Meg's mind raced off on a tangent, remembering how they'd hardly been able to keep their hands off each other back then. They'd willed lights to turn red so they could lean over and taste each other's lips at every intersection. Now they didn't even talk. In fact, the silence was so thick and heavy on the trip that Meg could barely breathe in the car with him.

Her hands longed to touch him, her lips to kiss him and her body to be taken by him, again and again. She glanced at him. He looked so cool, in dark trousers and a lemon polo shirt, that Meg wondered how long she'd be able to keep her hands to herself. She would have thought once was enough—or twice, or the three times last night—but it was as if she was addicted. She needed to get home as soon as she could.

Jake's twin-cab drew up to the kerb and Meg leapt from the car, dragging fresh, clean open air, untainted by Jake's presence or his heady aftershave, into her lungs.

A tape-recorder was thrust into her face. 'Is this your latest lover, Ms James?'

Meg's gaze snapped up and she looked into grey empty eyes that bedded deep into a man's skull as though they were crouching defensively from the world at large. Judging by the not-so-neat pile of cigarette butts near the low wall, he'd been waiting for hours for her to return.

'Is he?' he questioned insistently.

She could feel Jake's eyes on her as she perused the man. The name on his lapel was familiar. Meg squirmed inside. 'No!' She could feel the heat rise in her cheeks at the thought of her most personal, most intimate concerns being printed. Her life was *not* going to become a marketable commodity. It wasn't any business of the press or the public what she did with Jake. 'I'm not going to discuss anything with you. Not here. Not now. Make an appointment.'

'I did, Ms James, and you've cancelled it—four times!' the man wheezed. 'You stayed the night at his apartment.' He scrutinised her from head to foot, as if she had what she'd done written somewhere on her body.

She cringed. 'He's just a friend. An old friend.'

The man shrugged and twisted to Jake's rigid form. 'Mr Adams, how do you feel about being in the shadow of Megan's career?'

Jake glared at the man, his innards twisting sharply at the words Meg had used so casually—the same words she'd spoken that first day at the restaurant. Friends. He threw out his chest and stepped past the jerk, refusing to answer.

'Are you the father of her child?'

Jake stopped short.

'No!' Meg snapped, her cheeks flushed and her brow drawn. 'How dare you ask him that? How dare you ask anyone that?'

Jake's gut lurched. Why didn't she just tell the reporter and get it over with? It wasn't as if it was something the guy couldn't find out himself, given a bit of detective work. She'd be better off telling the truth than have him fill any holes in his story with pure fiction.

The man was light on his feet.

He was in front of Meg again, shoving the small recording device into her face. 'Then would *you* like to tell the world who the little kid's dad is?'

Meg tried to push past the man, her teeth clenched, but her breath came heavily, as if she was on the verge of tears.

'Ms James…?' the man pressed.

Jake's entire body reacted. He yanked the reporter back by his shirt. 'You leave her alone, mate,' he bit out, lacing every word with anger. He let go of the guy so suddenly that the reporter staggered to catch his balance.

Jake strode to catch up to Meg at the lifts. She stood with her arms folded tightly across her breasts, her feet moving restlessly on the floor as she watched the lift's progress on the lit panel above its doors, her cheeks ominously damp.

He touched her arm gently and she pulled away from him, piercing him with cold savage eyes. She stabbed the already lit button for the lift several more times.

He wanted to take her in his arms. If only she wasn't so stubbornly proud. He could kiss away her pain and solve everything for her. If she let him.

'What was that about? Who else are they suggesting is Tommy's father?' He couldn't help himself. He had to know. 'Have there been many men in your life?'

She cast him a long hard look. 'They make all sorts of things up.' The lift chimed its arrival. Meg stepped in and twisted to face him.

'And what about me and Tommy?' Was she ashamed of him being the father to their child, her husband? He straightened his shirt, his feet stumbling as he entered the lift. Wasn't he good enough for her yet?

She punched his floor number with a vengeance. 'You want your name plastered all over the papers?'

'Yes.' Jake turned and looked straight ahead at the shiny metallic doors. He didn't want to look at her. Didn't want to remind himself in any way that this woman, who he knew so well, who loved his body so well, who was the mother of his child, still hated him.

Meg raised her fine eyebrows. 'Why?'

'Why wouldn't I want the world to know I have a son?' Jake wanted to shout it from the biggest crane in Brisbane, from the top of Uluru, have a skywriter scrawl it over Sydney harbour against the brilliant blue sky.

'They'd find out about our marriage and want to know why I left you.'

Jake faltered. That would be juicy for the paper's circulation—a supposed philandering workaholic hubby with a drinking problem— and his mother and best mate would deliver it all to the nosy reporter on a platter. It hadn't taken Meg much encouragement to accept it. He figured the story would make a bestseller or a hit movie, with all its lies, betrayal and sex.

'Would you like to have everyone know you married me out of duty and obligation?' Meg punched the number of his floor again with such ferocity it was a wonder she didn't break it.

His gut rolled. 'It wasn't like that.'

'Oh, and lust.'

Jake dug his nails into his palms. She couldn't have made her feelings clearer. She hadn't listened to a word he'd told her.

The doors slid open. He cleared his throat. 'What about the other men in your life?' He *was* still her husband…

She grimaced at him and turned on her heel, heading straight for his apartment door. 'What men?' she tossed over her shoulder scornfully.

His heart jumped. 'You haven't been with anyone since me?' The thought cheered him. It explained why she'd been so wanton last night and so distant this morning. She'd wanted him and taken him. That was all there was to it. And he was the only one she'd chosen for the job. He smiled. He could handle that.

She spun back towards him, her hands on her hips, her cheeks flushed and her mouth pulled tight. 'And when in hell do you think I had time for men? I've been too busy trying to make a living and have a baby. Just surviving day to day was all I could manage for months on end.'

It was like a slap to the face. He'd missed out on it all. Watching her belly grow with the life inside her, helping her through the birth, late nights and dirty nappies—he'd lost it all.

She glared icily at him.

And he'd lost Meg too.

CHAPTER FIFTEEN

MEG swung open his front door. 'I'm sorry I haven't notched up a dozen guys on the bedhead so you feel more comfortable with yourself...' She twisted around to search his face, to see his reaction to her words.

'And what am I supposed to be sorry for?' Jake snarled. 'For getting on with my life after my wife disappeared on me?' He hesitated in the outside hall, giving his door a strange look as if it had suddenly turned alien.

'You call *keeping our house* getting on with your life? Heck, you haven't even had anyone living in it.' She pushed into the entry. 'You're living in denial, Jacob Adams, and the sooner you face it the better.'

'Face what?' His voice sounded dangerous, and he was right behind her. 'Denial of what, exactly?'

Meg swallowed hard. She had no idea what to say.

He stepped closer to her, then looked back at the open door. 'I locked it.'

Meg darted a look at the door in question and mulled over whether she'd turned the handle or just pushed it open. She definitely hadn't unlocked it. Her breath stuck in her lungs.

Jake stepped forward and wrapped a hand around Meg, drawing her close to his warm back. Her heart fluttered wildly in her breast, her hands hot and itching to touch his hard body.

'It seems I've come at a bad time.' The woman's voice was vaguely familiar.

Meg stepped out from behind her protector, her body going cold. Moira Adams, Jake's mother, was getting up off the couch. Just great—just what she needed!

The woman's hair was yet another different shade. The woman had always changed her hair as often as her shoes, and it appeared she still did.

She would've been pretty once, but hard lines from hard times hadn't done any justice to her features. She hadn't fared any better over the last three years—her mouth pinched and sullen, her eyes cool and assessing, her nose turned high.

Jake dropped his protective arm. 'What are you doing here, Mother? And how did you get in?' His eyes were dark and insolent as he moved towards the woman who'd brought him into the world.

Meg could tell instantly their relationship hadn't improved over time. Jake was still as upset and disgusted with his mother now as he had been as a teenager, with her slapdash approach to life, love and motherhood. From the stories she'd heard around the street, Jake was lucky to have survived growing up with the woman at all.

'I showed the superintendent three forms of ID proving I was your mother to get in here, so I could spend more than two minutes on the phone with my only child.' She stared pointedly at Meg. 'I wanted to see what was keeping you so busy.'

'Well, it's a lovely surprise. But not a convenient time, as you can see.' Jake waved a hand in Meg's direction, his whole body stiff.

Silence descended as Moira eyed Meg dubiously.

Jake paced the floor.

Meg guessed he was trying to expel some of the pent-up energy his mother evoked in him—the sort that could leave holes in walls if Jake were a violent man.

Meg felt Moira's eyes skitter over her, and she couldn't help but shift the weight on her feet nervously. Her suit was looking a bit the worse for wear, having been in and out of the car more times than a suit could possibly endure well.

She must look a wreck. But Meg resisted the urge to straighten her clothes and tidy her hair. Gone were the days when she'd been a young naive scared girl; now she was a scared woman, who was hell-bent on not showing one iota of fear to Jake's mother.

'Just like old times, isn't it?' Moira sauntered towards Meg with a confidence that had always reduced Meg to a pliable mass at the woman's feet.

Not this time.

Meg ground her teeth together. She straightened tall and held her ground. She could see Jake watching the both of them, and had the satisfaction of seeing him cringe. It looked for a moment as if he was going to leap between them.

'I guess, then, since you're here, that my son hasn't divorced you yet?' Moira eyed Meg scornfully. 'So you finally got to figuring you were on to a good thing and wanted him back?' Moira's voice was cutting and harsh, designed to stab right to her core.

'Mother!' Jake raked his fingers through his hair and stepped forward. 'It's not like that.'

'We're only friends, Mrs Adams.' Meg remained calm, letting the spite slide off her back. She had no reason to quarrel with this woman or even seek approval from her—Jake and her were over. Moira couldn't hurt her any more.

'Very friendly friends, from what I can see. I'm not blind, Megan.'

'I don't know what you are.' Jake stepped between them. 'But you seem to be missing the point, as usual.'

'And what's that supposed to mean?'

'You don't seem to see clearly when Meg's around.'

Meg could agree with that. She figured she ought to step out from behind Jake, but it was a novel experience to have someone in her corner—especially Jake. He hadn't been around much for anything much at all, except bedtime. She felt the heat rise in her cheeks—better not to dwell on that aspect of their relationship with his strong hard back inches from her, his cologne tantalising her nostrils and a heat emanating from his body that called directly to hers.

'Really? Well, I can't imagine why I don't like the girl,' she bit out sarcastically. 'Nothing to do with her not even giving me the time of day.'

'I think you're confusing Meg with her father.'

Meg froze. What did her father have to do with anything? Sure, Moira hadn't appreciated her coming into Jake's life, but Meg had always figured she resented her for not being good enough for her son, that she wanted more than the girl next door for an in-law. Why bring her father into it?

'I'll have you know *he* loved me, but *I* wouldn't have a bar of him.' Moira's voice rose in pitch.

Meg stepped out from behind Jake and stared at the woman. How could she be so delusional? Her father had disliked her. He'd seen her for what she was—a good time waiting to happen on a man's bank balance.

Meg had never had her own opinion on the woman. She had to admit she hadn't been able to see much past Jake in those days. And now... Meg cocked her head and ran her eyes over Moira Adams. Her corn-colored hair sat atop her head in ringlets that were an obvious attempt at creating the illusion of innocence and youth, which was hard to keep up with her heavy make-up desperately covering her wrinkles. But it was up to Moira how she lived her life, and what friends, enemies and men she had in it.

'You have a grandson, Moira,' Meg offered gently.

'What?' Her eyes flew wide, her false lashes slapping against her eyebrows. She twisted to her son, her voice laced with accusation. 'I thought you said it was Dan's.'

'I was an idiot.'

Meg could agree there. A silly fool who'd listened to lies. Her mind screeched to a halt—*just as she had done three years ago*. She'd listened to what everyone had said to her and done all this to herself and Jake. Realisation knotted in her chest. She was to blame for the last three years too. If she'd had more trust, more faith in him and herself, things would've turned out differently.

'Show me a photo, girl.' Moira thrust her hand, palm upward, in front of Meg, her finely manicured stick-on nails painted a garish purple that contrasted terribly against the lemon suit she wore.

Meg scrambled in her purse. She finally handed a photo to Moira, avoiding looking at Jake. She could feel him watching her, as if he was willing her to look at him, so he could tell her something with his eyes. But she wasn't about to look—she had a fair idea of the vibes he was shooting her way and they weren't conducive to her staying in control.

'Oh, my.' Moira's eyes glistened. 'He looks just like you...' She swung to Jake and gave him a firm slap to his face. 'How could you mistake him?' Moira looked at Meg and swallowed hard. 'I'm so sorry, Megan. For everything I've said and done. I'm just a foolish, selfish woman.'

She saw Jake roll his eyes as his mother hugged her.

It felt strange to hold Jake's mother. She'd never had the opportunity to feel how hard and bony the woman was under the layers of clothes she wore. It somehow made her more real, even though the hug only lasted a moment.

'I'll leave you two to it, then.' Moira stepped back to the lounge and plucked up her purple furred handbag.

'There's no *it*, Moira,' Meg assured her. She didn't want the woman to get the wrong idea and be disappointed. There wasn't a chance in hell that Meg was going to let *it* happen again tonight.

Moira made a guttural noise in her throat, a smile tugging at the corners of her crimson lipstick. 'When are you coming back north? I'd love to see the little boy.'

Meg shook her head. 'I've no idea if I'm coming up again, Moira. But you can come to Melbourne any time to see Tommy.'

'I meant when are you *moving* up? Jake can't go leaving his company and waltz down south. Besides, I'm a great babysitter.'

'I think you've misunderstood.' Meg looked to Jake for help, but it was as though he was enjoying her discomfort and his mother's bluntness.

Meg felt the air was suddenly thicker; drawing it into her lungs was an effort. She was losing control here. They were taking over! She suddenly saw her well-ordered, independent life flying off into the sunset. She clenched her hands into fists, not about to let it slide. 'I may have married your son and had his child, but that doesn't mean I'm going to drop everything that's important to me for him. I'm sorry if that sounds harsh, but that's the way it is!'

'Fine. No need to get so personal. I'll see you soon, then.' She winked at her son and sauntered to the door. 'And if you don't know what to get me for my birthday you can make me one of those full-length numbers from the fashion show.'

Meg's mouth dropped open. She would love to advise Moira on her wardrobe, but thinking she'd give her a four-thousand-dollar dress for her birthday was pushing relations a little far.

The door closed behind Mrs Adams, shutting out the world and emphasising Jake's larger than life presence in the room. Her body ached for him, her throat ached, and all she wanted to do was cry all the tears she'd held pent up for him over the last three years.

She stepped back, increasing the distance between them. 'I'm going home, Jake.'

He swung around to her. 'You can't. You still have appointments.'

She bit her inner lip until she tasted the sweet saltiness of blood. He was right. Damn him. She had to stay until it was over. But then that was it. She was out of there before her traitorous body did anything else she would regret.

Their eyes locked and a shudder passed through her. His eyes were as dark and as powerful as he was, and she was adrift in dangerous waves of emotion.

Visions of meeting more strangers came to mind. 'No, say an emergency came up and I'll send them a proposal.'

'Sounds like you're running away again.'

'There's nothing wrong with running away.' It was safer that way. That way her heart would have a chance. If she stayed she'd be broken again.

He gazed at her speculatively.

She lifted her chin in defiance. 'Fine, I'll stick around. But you keep your hands and eyes off me.'

He raised his eyebrows, a smile tugging at the corners of his sensuous mouth.

Meg's heart turned over. 'And don't do that either.'

Jake shrugged and sauntered across the room, staring out of one of the floor-to-ceiling windows. He stood there a moment in silence. 'What about dinner?'

'What about it?' Meg snapped, inching backwards to her room. 'You want to order pizza?' There was no way she was going to suggest beans. She knew where they led. She'd be lucky if she was ever going to be able to look at another bean in her life without images of Jake and their lovemaking popping into her mind.

'No.' Jake turned to her. 'Let's go out.' He was cool and casual, and any sensuality she'd caught in his eyes before had been swept aside.

Jake was up to something, and it was up to her to keep her head clear and above water, stay away from those deep sensuous eyes that threatened to drown her.

'You might feel safer out, with lots of people around. I know this really nice restaurant at Southbank.' Jake shoved his hands into his pockets. 'Great food.'

'A restaurant sounds good. But I'm not scared of you, you know,' she tossed over her shoulder bravely as she walked into her room. She thought she heard Jake laugh as she closed the door. The nerve of the man!

The restaurant was gorgeous. Deep red drapes hung at each of the eight-foot-high windows looking out over the river with the lights of the city on the other side. The tablecloths matched, and the soft candlelight was mood-inducing in the softly lit room. The music was live, the musicians walking around with violins and guitars, singing love songs to the people already at the tables.

'Jake!' she reproached, swinging to him. He looked incredible in a black suit and tie, his every curve, his every muscle calling to Meg.

'You have a problem?' His eyes glinted mischievously.

Meg averted her gaze. She would have to keep her eyes in check as well as her body. It wouldn't do to give Jake the wrong idea, and judging by the dark gleam in his eyes he had that all right. 'Yes, I have a problem. How about we go to McDonalds?'

'Why?' He took her hand and led her to the *maître d'*, his roguish smile firmly in place, his warm hand enveloping hers, and his thumb tracing the soft skin of the back of her hand with such tenderness that her body couldn't help but respond.

This was the Jake she knew. The man she'd loved and married. The man that could sweep her away with a look, with a word, with a kiss. Jake was no longer the brooding dark ex—she was in real trouble now.

'This is an intimate setting designed to induce people into jumping into bed. We don't want that.'

Jake moved closer to Meg, as if reading her thoughts. 'Don't we?' His voice was soft and alarming. 'Didn't you have a good time last night?'

An unwelcome heat crept into her cheeks and her body tingled in remembrance. 'That's not the point!'

He leant close to her and breathed into her ear. 'What *is* the point?'

Meg pulled away from him.

The *maître d'* stood in front of them, twirling an impossibly fine, long moustache. He wore a black suit and a bow tie and was impatiently indicating for them to follow him.

Meg concentrated on weaving through the tables after the penguin, trying to keep her mind in control and not on the six feet of hunky male trailing after her. When the man stopped, Meg almost ploughed into him.

'Your seat, madam.' He pulled out her chair.

'Allow me.' Jake almost shoved the poor penguin out of the way to hang onto her seat.

Meg cleared her throat and pretended not to be affected. 'You don't have to do that.' She wondered whether he was being gallant or if he was going to pull it out from under her as she sat. She darted a glance at him as she lowered herself into the chair. A perfect gentleman.

She followed Jake with her eyes as he made his way to his side of the table and sat down.

'What?' His mouth curved into a smile.

Meg knew he had a fair idea of what was going through her mind. She dropped her gaze to her napkin and involved herself with placing it over her lap. Her hands fumbled and she decided it would be best to keep them out of sight.

'You look beautiful.'

Meg snapped her attention to him. His eyes shone with approval. His gaze dropped from her tousled hair to her neck and over her breasts, modestly covered by the full-length black satin gown she wore. A myriad of overlapping fine straps covered her otherwise bare shoulders, keeping the whole creation from falling to her feet which, by the looks of it, was exactly where Jake would have preferred it.

The waiter offered a bottle of wine for Jake to peruse. He nodded at the label, casting Meg a boyish look as it was poured. Jake picked up the glass carefully, theatrically throwing out his little finger as he raised it to his mouth. He smacked and pouted his lips, sloshing the contents around for almost a minute, all the while pulling faces at Meg, before finally swallowing it.

Meg suppressed a grin. The waiter poured hers, looking a little less pleased and less patient after Jake's performance. Looking at Jake now, she could almost forget the last few years. *Almost.*

The waiter bowed and left, leaving Meg staring at the hazy words of the menu, unable to concentrate at all.

'So...?' Jake stared across at Meg.

'What?' Meg felt there was definitely something more going on with Jake than just dinner.

'You've spoken to my mother and now have a fair idea she would have said anything to upset you—to get back, in some really weird way, at your father.'

'So?' Meg swallowed nervously. She knew where this was heading and her stomach was a massing squall of nerves.

'And you now know that Danny really liked you and said what he said out of jealousy.'

'He *could* have,' Meg qualified. She hadn't come straight out and asked him whether he'd deliberately lied to her to sabotage her marriage to Jake, but from what had gone on in Melbourne with him it was more than likely.

'Meg, you and I owe it to Tommy to give this another chance.' Jake reached his hand over the table and laid it next to her glass.

Meg clenched her own hands together, staring into Jake's face as if she could scry deep into his soul and see whether he'd matured, whether he told the truth, before she placed her hand in his, her life in his.

'Would you like to order now?'

Jake shot a steely glare at the guy and looked positively murderous at the interruption. He ignored the waiter and set his eyes on Meg. 'Chicken?' Jake murmured.

'What?' It had the exact lilt of the taunt he'd used to harass her with to get her to do some crazy dangerous thing. 'Chicken?' Her pride stirred deep within her, shooting up to meet the challenge head-on.

'The lady wishes for chicken?'

'No,' Jake offered. 'The lady *is* chicken.'

Meg glanced at the waiter's face, which had fallen from cordiality to wide-eyed concern. He shifted restlessly, probably not sure whether to hold his ground and stave off a fight or to run for cover.

Meg glared at Jake. A smile pulled at the corners of his mouth. She kicked him under the table and had the satisfaction of seeing the pain on his face. 'I'll have the chicken Parmigiana and a salad. No soup and no dessert.'

'Don't you feel you deserve some sweetness in your life?' Jake prodded, putting his menu down and picking up his wine.

'Thank you,' she bit out to Jake, 'but I know what I want.'

'Do you?' Jake pushed, searching her eyes.

'Yes.' Her voice wavered annoyingly.

The waiter coughed. 'And you, sir?'

Jake looked at the man blankly for a moment, then waved his hand dismissively. 'Smoked salmon and salad.'

The waiter almost ran from their table and Meg couldn't help but break into a smile. It was nerves, she was sure.

'No sweet?' she teased Jake, trying to lighten the mood between them.

'I have all the sweetness any man could possibly ever want right in front of me.'

Meg stared at her hands in her lap. 'Jake…'

'What do *you* want, Meg?' Jake's voice held a tremor of excitement.

She snapped her mouth shut, stunned by his bluntness. She hadn't expected it—had virtually relied on him not being totally honest with her. Games she could handle. Honesty and baring the soul—no way.

'I want to go to the ladies' room.' She needed more than thirty seconds to figure out an answer to his question that didn't lay her heart on the railway tracks, ready for the next train.

He eyed her carefully, standing up as she stood, moving closer to her before she could run. 'Give it a chance, Meg. You can trust me.'

Dabbing powder onto her face wasn't a crash-hot distraction from her problem, but Meg slapped her face with the small round blotter, trying to cover the red slashes on her cheeks. She wanted Jake. Had wanted him since she was twelve. And now he was offering himself. Meg had no idea on what terms, but she was coming to the conclusion she wasn't ever going to escape the excruciating pain of loving the guy. And she might have a chance of happy-ever-after if she could bring herself to take the risk…

Meg shoved her make-up back into her small handbag and gave herself what she hoped was a confidence-boosting smile. She didn't have to answer now. She could question Jake further on exactly what he had in mind before she had to make any commitment.

'Why, Megan J, what a surprise,' a sophisticated musical voice lilted.

Meg stared into the mirror and a tall woman slowly came into focus at the rear of the room. Vivian! She turned reluctantly. 'Why, hello. Fancy meeting you here.'

'It's my favourite restaurant.' She approached the mirror, flicking her impossibly long black hair over her shoulder and taking out her compact. 'I come here all the time.'

Meg's optimism dropped to her toes. 'That's nice.' Jake couldn't possibly have brought her to one of Vivian's haunts… She reached into her bag and pulled out a mint, placing it in her mouth.

'How did you go with those investors?' Vivian leant close to the mirror and painted her lips crimson, to match her dress.

'Pardon?' Meg almost choked.

Vivian was in no hurry. She puckered her lips and smacked them together, distributing the colour evenly. 'The people to invest in your label that I lined up for Jacob.'

She felt ice spreading through her body. '*You* did?'

'Yes, of course. Didn't he tell you?' Vivian lowered her lashes. 'Oh, dear. I hope I haven't put my foot in it.'

'Not at all.' Meg's throat closed over. She backed out through the door, her eyes gliding over Vivian's elegance and perfection. She'd been kidding herself. Jake hadn't changed. He was still a liar!

CHAPTER SIXTEEN

'WHAT do you think you were doing? I would have driven you back.' Jake shoved the key in the lock of his apartment door and pushed it open.

Meg cringed. His anger was palpable. Of course he was right. It had been foolish to run off in a taxi when he was there with the car, but she'd needed space from him. Room to think. Sanity to bless her with inspiration on what she could do to escape this mess.

She couldn't look at him.

'Why did you run off without telling me? My suggestion wasn't that repulsive to you, was it?'

'I came to the sudden realisation that I don't want to continue.' She bit out the words, willing her body to stop shaking. 'I don't want to be anywhere near you, okay?'

Jake's shoulders sagged and his voice lowered dangerously. 'And what about what I want?'

'I don't need this, Jake. I have nothing more to say to you.' She stormed down the hall and into her room and slammed the door. She snatched up the phone and ordered another taxi, then threw her clothes into her bag.

It wasn't as though she was chicken. She just wasn't going to waste her breath explaining to Jake that she'd run into Vivian and she'd spilt the beans—that he was obviously still on with her.

Meg knew it was rash to leave the other investors hanging, but if the people she'd spoken to today all came through she was out of the woods. Mrs Bolton would have her money and her boutique would be very nicely and safely set up.

Meg slammed the case shut. Jake wasn't a long-term proposition—he wasn't even a short one. Vivian's revelation had driven that home. Knowing Jake, he probably still felt obliged to her father to look after her. Damn him. And damn her father.

Meg burst from the room. Jake was sitting at the table, a daily paper laid out in front of him, a cup of coffee full to the brim beside it. There wasn't any steam rising from it; there had to be about as little warmth in it as in Jake's eyes.

He cast a cold glare at her suitcase but didn't move.

She bit her inner lip. She *was* doing the right thing. 'I'm going. Send me the names of the other investors and I'll make sure they get a proposal.'

Jake didn't say a word. His eyes were like bits of stone and it was all she could do to resist the urge to go to him.

Meg marched to the door resolutely, holding her breath. She knew that if he turned on the charm she would melt into his arms and beg him to kiss away the past, her father, his promise and all her responsibilities.

She grabbed the cool hard metal of the doorhandle.

'Sometimes when you hold out for everything you get nothing.' Jake's voice was thick and unsteady and cut through her thoughts like a blade in butter.

She faltered for only a moment. Was she holding out for everything? She closed the door behind her. More importantly, was she going to end up with nothing?

Meg dropped her head onto her desk, delighting in the loud thump and the accompanying pain to match that in her heart. Jake's words had stuck with her, worming their way deep into her mind, taunting her as the days and weeks dragged by. She felt alone. More alone than she'd ever felt.

The door flung open and Suzie burst in, Joyce following close on her heels. 'I'm so sorry, Megan. I know you said no calls or interruptions, but she got past me.'

Suzie propped herself on the edge of Meg's desk. 'You haven't returned my calls or seen me for over a month!' She peered at the empty desk in front of Meg. 'So what is it? Working hard or feeling sorry for yourself?'

Meg gave Suzie a dark look. 'As a matter of fact—' Meg pulled out some documents from the drawer '—I was just starting...'

'Yeah? Then who whacked you in the head?'

Meg gingerly touched her forehead. It was more than a little numb. 'There's a mark?'

'As if you'd slapped some beetroot on it, or missed with the blusher, or banged your head against a wall. You know they mean that figuratively, not literally.' Suzie laughed. 'Don't tell me—you're having trouble with your hubby.'

Meg snapped her attention to Suzie. 'I didn't tell you that.'

'I had a chat with that Dan guy, and I know why you ran away from that gorgeous hunk and why you're banging walls with your head.' She leant closer to Meg. 'Look, if you don't take a chance you'll end up an old spinster, like that great-aunt Winnie of yours.'

'But what about that Vivian woman?'

'Don't worry about her. Jake wants you! He got her involved to try and save your marriage.' Suzie picked up a pencil off Meg's desk and chewed the end. 'I had a long chat with her too, you know.'

Meg straightened. 'When? About what?'

Suzie looked to the ceiling. 'Everything. Just after you told Jake Tommy was his. She cornered me at the store.'

'About Mrs Bolton pulling her funds?' Meg held her breath and prayed.

'Yep. Everything.'

Meg covered her mouth as her heart leapt. Suzie had told Vivian about Meg's financial difficulties and Vivian had genuinely tried to help. Meg had distrusted Jake before without reason, and now she'd done it again! Hadn't she learned anything about the last three years?

'So, how about it?' Suzie slid the pencil back into the holder and smiled. 'Are you going to give it a go?'

'What if he doesn't want me? What happens if he hurts me again?' Meg huddled defensively against the notion. 'I couldn't bear to see rejection in his eyes.'

'We all take that chance every time we talk to a man.' Suzie put a hand on her shoulder. 'I guess the real question is, do you love him?'

Meg looked down at the file, her stomach twisting.

'Do you want me to go and shake some sense into him again?'

'No.' Meg straightened herself in her chair. 'I'm a strong, independent businesswoman and—'

'Yeah, right. You're a wuss. A very talented creative wuss, but a wuss all the same. Heck, if you didn't have hard-nosed Joyce out there, taking care of the rough and tumble business side of things, you'd be stuffed.'

Meg glared at Suz. 'Just humour me, will you?'

Suzie shrugged. 'Okay, you're going to take care of Jake all by yourself.' She leant closer. 'So what are you going to do, exactly?' Suzie looked at her watch and leapt off Meg's desk.

'Gotta go—or I'll be late for work. Give me a call about it— I don't bite!'

Meg stared at the door after Suzie had gone and then at the phone. It was time she took her life firmly into her own hands. Her pulse jerked into full speed, her heart thudded against her ribcage, her lips went dry. She picked up the handpiece and punched the numbers from the notepad shaking in her other hand.

Jake stomped through the mud. The wet had finally broken and had stuffed up his job totally. He should have taken a sand job, then the rain would have been a bloody blessing not a curse.

The guys were in the crib shed having a break. Jake stepped into the shelter they huddled in at breaks. The steel floor was more mud than metal and the air more smoke and sweat than air. The faint aroma of coffee could just be made out in the stench.

'Congrats, mate.' The foreman grabbed Jake's hand and shook it vigorously. 'Didn't know you had it in ya.'

Jake shook his head. Had the guys been drinking? The smirks and nudges of the six guys in the shed reeked of conspiracy. Something more than the rain had to be going down.

'I don't understand...?'

The foreman thrust his newspaper at Jake. He didn't know whether to read it or clean his boots with it. He eyed the guy he thought he knew pretty well with a new perspective. Crazy season?

One of the labourers jumped up and stabbed at a picture of a woman on the page and realisation dawned on Jake. They were ogling someone.

His eyes focused on the smiling deep blue eyes, the short golden hair and familiar full lips. His heart lurched in his chest. Meg! And Tommy was with her, in her arms. He wore overalls and a miniature yellow hard hat.

The foreman stepped forward and read over Jake's shoulder, '"*Melbourne designer finds hubby*".' He sniggered. 'And guess what? It's you. It says that you were married over three years ago and work had gotten between you two and she left.' The guy slapped Jake on the shoulder. 'Happens a lot, mate.'

'Too right,' said another. 'Construction's a hard mistress.'

'I wouldn't have taken it over that dish in the paper, though.' He cast a look of incredulity at Jake. 'I woulda stayed close to the home fires, if ya know what I mean.'

Jake snatched the paper back and scanned the article. It said a lot about her designs and about her boutique. He held his breath.

When asked whether her recent outings with her estranged husband, Jacob Adams, indicated a resolution to the rift, Megan J answered with a smile. 'We have a lot of things to work out but I'm sure there's hope at the end of the tunnel as long as we both don't hold out for everything.'

Jake left the shed at a run, the paper clenched firmly in his hand.

'What about the job?' one of the guys called.

Jake didn't give a damn. All that mattered was getting to Meg, and this time he was going to get it right.

CHAPTER SEVENTEEN

JAKE crashed through her door without warning. Joyce stood behind him, face pale and eyes wide with a concern Meg hadn't seen since she had thrown up into her bin last week at the strong odour of some new fabric samples.

'It's okay, Joyce.' Meg stood up. Jake looked vibrant, but worn. There was an excited light in his eyes and Meg almost felt guilty for the candid interview she'd done with the reporter.

Her legs felt weak and she moved over to the sofa, settling in the seat before looking at Jake. She willed the calm she'd been practising since the interview, two days ago, to come back to her.

He rubbed his jeans with the palms of his hands and paced the floor. 'I saw the paper. I guess I have to ask if what they said was how you said it. You know—not twisted or warped or taken out of context or anything.' He turned and stood rigid, awaiting her response.

Meg's heart skipped a beat, then thudded madly. 'You could have rung to ask.'

Jake's expression dimmed and he shifted his weight back and forth from foot to foot. 'You mean they misquoted you? Made it all up?' His voice rose an octave.

'No.' A warm glow spread from her heart to her toes. 'I was very specific about what sort of litigation I would shove where if they even got one word wrong.'

Jake smiled, his whole being morphing. He reduced the distance between them and dropped to his knees in front of her. 'Meg.' Her name was a whisper on his lips. He thrust a hand into his pocket and pulled something out.

He flattened his palm, looking into her eyes. A gold band lay against his skin. *Her old ring.* She covered her mouth to smother the surprise. 'You kept it?'

'Yes.'

'Why?' she croaked.

'Because I couldn't let you go.'

Meg stiffened. *Let you go*, she repeated to herself. *Let—give permission.* 'I'm not some prize you can win, then ferret away somewhere and not worry about,' she snarled, wondering what sort of idiot she was. He wasn't going to change—he was a male chauvinist pig and he wasn't going to take over her life again.

'It wasn't like that.' Jake's voice was harsh. 'You were never a prize.'

'No, I was a freebie. Given by my father and eagerly accepted as a dutiful responsibility to the man you worshipped.' Tears clogged her throat and burnt her eyes.

Jake's face darkened and he rose without another word. He strode to the door.

Her heart squeezed tight and her breath stuck in her throat. This couldn't keep happening to them. If there was a chance for them they'd have to let go of the past, and she knew it was her that was stuck in it. Tears menaced her eyes. 'Jake.' Her voice was no more than a hoarse whisper.

He froze, his stance rigid, not even turning to face her.

She swallowed her pride. 'If you love me, now is the time to tell me.' It was all that mattered. It didn't matter that she loved *him*—because if he didn't love her... He'd be miserable. They'd make each other miserable. A life without love was no life at all.

He turned, and his eyes had a faraway burning in them. 'What?'

Her heart sank to her toes. 'Nothing...' She couldn't say it again. Couldn't bring herself to repeat it while he watched her, while she could see the indifference in his eyes.

He was suddenly at her feet, kneeling before her, grasping her hands in his. 'Meg, I love you. Of course I love you. It nearly broke my heart in two when I came home to find you gone. I figured you'd felt smothered, that I forced you into a marriage you didn't want.'

'But the promise to my father—'

He shrugged. 'It was a good excuse to marry you. But he only wanted me to look out for you.' He looked up into her eyes. 'Forgive me for not coming after you. I was a fool.'

'Yes,' she breathed. 'Do you really love me? You're not just saying it so you can get me into your bed again?'

His eyes twinkled, then he sobered. 'I love you, Meg. Only you.' His lips touched hers in a feather-light caress that shook her to the very core of her being. She surrendered to him, to his lips, and let him sweep her into the warmth of his arms.

'Jake, there's something I have to tell you.' She took a breath. 'I'm pregnant.' The test this morning had confirmed her suspicions. Trust her to be so fertile. He probably could have just glanced at her with one of those sexy burning looks and done it.

She'd almost come to terms with it. With the extra backers for her business she'd be in a position to employ a manager for the boutique, so she'd be able to lessen her workload for the baby. She mentally crossed her fingers, praying she'd have the new baby and Jake too.

'Whose is it?'

Meg's heart lurched up her throat, her hand flying of its own accord and connecting with Jake's face.

'I was kidding.' Jake grinned, ignoring his reddening cheek and sweeping her into his arms. He kissed her again soundly. 'There's nothing I want more than to see my baby grow inside the woman I love.'

Meg punched him in the shoulder. 'I don't appreciate your brand of humour.'

'Do you appreciate me?' His voice was silky and seductive. 'Do you *love* me?'

'Hmm, let me count the ways,' she murmured, running her hands up inside his shirt and along his bare skin.

MILLS & BOON® PUBLISH EIGHT LARGE PRINT TITLES A MONTH. THESE ARE THE EIGHT TITLES FOR DECEMBER 2002

THE HONEYMOON CONTRACT
Emma Darcy

ETHAN'S TEMPTRESS BRIDE
Michelle Reid

HIS CONVENIENT MARRIAGE
Sara Craven

THE ITALIAN'S TROPHY MISTRESS
Diana Hamilton

THE FIANCÉ FIX
Carole Mortimer

BRIDE BY DESIGN
Leigh Michaels

THE WHIRLWIND WEDDING
Day Leclaire

HER MARRIAGE SECRET
Darcy Maguire

MILLS & BOON®

1102 Rom LP

MILLS & BOON® PUBLISH EIGHT LARGE PRINT TITLES A MONTH. THESE ARE THE EIGHT TITLES FOR JANUARY 2003

❧

A PASSIONATE SURRENDER
Helen Bianchin

THE HEIRESS BRIDE
Lynne Graham

HIS VIRGIN MISTRESS
Anne Mather

TO MARRY McALLISTER
Carole Mortimer

MISTAKEN MISTRESS
Margaret Way

THE BEDROOM ASSIGNMENT
Sophie Weston

THE PREGNANCY BOND
Lucy Gordon

A ROYAL PROPOSITION
Marion Lennox

MILLS & BOON®